Edward Everett Hale

**What Career?**

Ten papers on the choice of a vocation and the use of time

Edward Everett Hale

**What Career?**
*Ten papers on the choice of a vocation and the use of time*

ISBN/EAN: 9783337423704

Printed in Europe, USA, Canada, Australia, Japan

Cover: Foto ©Andreas Hilbeck / pixelio.de

More available books at **www.hansebooks.com**

# WHAT CAREER?

TEN PAPERS ON THE

## CHOICE OF A VOCATION AND THE USE OF TIME.

By E. E. HALE,

AUTHOR OF "HOW TO DO IT."

QUI LEGIT REGIT

BOSTON:
ROBERTS BROTHERS.
1878.

CAMBRIDGE:
PRESS OF JOHN WILSON AND SON.

TO

MY BRETHREN

OF

ALPHA DELTA PHI,

THIS VOLUME IS DEDICATED.

EDWARD E. HALE.

ROXBURY, MASS.,
December 17, 1877.

# CONTENTS.

# WHAT CAREER?

## I.

## THE LEADERS LEAD.

AN ADDRESS DELIVERED BEFORE THE CONVENTION OF ALPHA DELTA PHI, AT WILLIAMS COLLEGE, MAY 24, 1877.

WHO are the leaders of society, gentlemen, and how shall they be found?

This question, in one way or another, is of course at the bottom of all questions of government. As we live, it is often vaguely and often falsely answered, because people are misled by the analogies of European literature and history, — analogies which must deceive, in social conditions so utterly new as ours. Our President is not a king; our people is not a third estate; our churches are not hierarchies; our aristocracy is not hereditary. There is no resemblance between the duty of the governor of an American State and that

1

of the prefect of a French department or the lord-lieutenant of an English county. For such reasons, it becomes impossible to transfer from the older systems of government to our systems even the commonplaces, or what are called the axioms, of their political and social economy. And the attempt to make such transfer, on the part of half-trained writers, confuses and in the end embarrasses our administration of our own affairs. It is indeed the origin of half that pessimism which tells us in each hour that we are going to perdition. A prominent English writer said to me once: "Of course you know that there never was any thing we call a nation which extended from one ocean to another." I said: "I know it very well; but our exact business is to show that what we call a nation can extend from one ocean to the other." But I had to add, that "what we call a nation is something world-wide apart from what you call a nation, and that is the reason why you never understand us." I might have added, I suppose, "why we never understand you."

This sort of vagueness, not to say misapprehension, affects the question, Who are our Leaders; where are they at work, and how are they to be found? Thomas Carlyle — the especial absolutist of our time — growls out his dissatisfaction with all democratic systems of finding leaders. Other grumblers and growlers of his own nation, or of other nations, take up the easy refrain, and on the same or on another key repeat the dissatisfaction with what is. I am afraid that young men who read the journals much, not having yet found out the best ways of saving time, are apt to be unduly impressed by the weeping and wailing and gnashing of teeth of those writers for the press, who find nothing good outside the walls of their own offices. In the vain attempt to apply European precedents to American realities, such writers, especially if they have been educated abroad, tell us, week by week, that the Pope is quite wrong, and the Patriarch of the Greek Church equally wrong; that the Roman Catholic Church is wholly wrong, and that Protestantism is not worth mention; that

the Emperor of Russia is wrong, while the
Sultan was never right; that Count Bismark is
lamentably wrong, Marshal McMahon entirely
mistaken, and Mr. Disraeli and Mr. Gladstone
each as absurd as the other; that General Grant
was all wrong, and that Mr. Hayes is all
wrong; that no man of any sense cares for Governor Robinson or Governor Rice; and that
there is not a city in America which has any
notion of what government is or should be.
The oracles are dumb, the lamp of God has
burned out, — if indeed there be any God, which
they say is doubtful. There is no open vision.
From such moanings unutterable the educated
young men of America would sink back, de-
spairing, but that always in the same issue of
the same journal, whichever it may be, there
appears one gleam of golden hope. For it
seems that in that particular office, by the
united graces of natural selection, of evolution, and of accident, there is one clear fountain
of absolute truth and absolute wisdom. From
that office weekly will trickle forth rills of wise
direction, sufficient for one week for the salva-

tion of the land. If only the people will subscribe liberally to this particular journal, whichever it may be, all will be well!

Now it happens, in fact, that our fathers, of the era of the Revolution and the generation after,-relieved us from many of the European dangers and evils. Grant that we have many of our own: of course we have. Still it is a shame that we should be taught that the particular evils of Europe are on our shoulders; and that the great grievance of all in their affairs is a grievance in ours. The grievance in their affairs is doubtless what Carlyle says it is. "The man who *can*," he says, "is not king. He ought to be king. Canning, cunning, könig, — man who is able, — ought to be the man who reigns." You cannot say this is true, whether in England, in Germany, in Italy, or in Spain. You cannot say that the Prince of Wales, or the Emperor of Germany, or King Victor Emmanuel, or the King Alfonso is the ablest man in either country. If then you stick to the theory that the king is the ruler, you must own that the time is out of joint, and that the world has not hit on a good way to find its leaders. But when you come over to America, it is not the President who rules, it is not the governor of a State who rules. It is the people who rule. And though in England your mournful poet may sing of unknown

" Hands that the rod of empire might have swayed ; "

of " village Hampdens," or " inglorious Miltons," — it is by no means certain that we have any inglorious Miltons or village Hampdens. It is certain that our system attempts to keep open the lines of promotion, which the systems of the Old World generally try to close. Because we keep them open, — certainly so far as we keep them open, — we shall find the real correction and the truly conservative element in our affairs. I believe, gentlemen, that we shall find in our history, and in our present fortune, that

### THE LEADERS LEAD.

To justify this thesis will be my effort in this hour.

I. It will probably be found that in all history Mr. Canning's epigram is true, — that the horse drags the cart, and the cart does not push the horse along.   After the glamour of the time, — after the smoke and dust have passed away, history will probably always show that certain men and women, who, as the Book of Proverbs says, no man of their own time has much cared for, have still been they who have saved the city.   Even in those complicated arrangements of the Old World, your Napoleon and Cromwell, your Calvin and Luther, your Hildebrand and other Gregories, — men who were not born to thrones, — have a very uncomfortable way of tumbling thrones over, and, if they choose, erecting others in their places.   Take such a life as that of Bernard of Clairvaux.   Not long after William the Conqueror landed in England, Bernard was born in Burgundy.   A young man, he chose a monastic life.   A young man, only twenty-five years old, he chose twelve companions, and, with their spades and hoes on their shoulders, they marched into a wilderness of banditti to found a convent.   They separated themselves from all command, you say.

They sank into lazy and selfish seclusion.
That is because you take the word "king" as
being the only word that means "ruler." In
fact, Bernard was a born Leader. He could
not help leading. From the Wormwood valley
in which he settled, he called up the "Clara
Vallis," — the Clairvaux, — which was, for centuries, the centre of light to Europe. From that
centre he sent out like-organized emigration into
a hundred other centres of barbarism and plun-
der. Before he died, he was the centre of the
education of his time: and that meant the government, nay, it seems to have meant even the
agriculture and art, of his time. The little
kings referred their quarrels to this leader of
men. Conclave after conclave asked him to be
Pope. But he knew, as he said, that he was
more Pope than the Popes he made. Such a
man as that changes the social order of Europe,
introduces a new civilization, starts crusades on
their career whether of darkness or of light,
sets up kings, and throws them down. Yet
when you have to put him in a class, he is
neither emperor, king, duke, nor prince. He
is something much more than any one of them:

he is a Leader of men.  The Leader leads, and the "thrones, dominations, princedoms, virtues, powers," meekly and orderly obey.

But it is not my business to show that the Old World offers to all men alike the field and chance for a noble ambition.  The difficulties are legion which have been reared there, to prevent the man of native genius from making his way to the front.  And the contrivances are endless, as all the satirists show, by which incompetent men are bolstered up to power, — the lame pigeon, as Paley said, taking the rule of the flock.  I am very sorry for them.  But my business is not with them.  My effort now is to show that, thanks to the system to which we are born, which is so natural that we forget that it exists, these difficulties fall away with us, and these contrivances are futile.  With us the lines of promotion are open.  In that is the secret of our successes.  To keep them open is the first duty of our self-preservation.  Because they are open, and as long as they are kept open, with us

### THE LEADERS LEAD.

1*

There is a pathetic story of a lad named
MacDonald, who was born in Oregon ; and who,
before he was a man, was shipwrecked on the
shore of Japan. According to the cruel custom of the old government of that country, he
was caged, in the province where his life was
saved, and kept there as a prisoner indefinitely.
It was while he was so held, that an American
Commodore touched at Nagasaki, and in an
interview on the deck of his own ship was
struck by a Japanese official. The Japanese
government was alarmed. They wanted to
know just what they had done ; and they sent
for young MacDonald to ask what was the
grade of a commodore ; — how many grades of
officers were below him. He told them, with
precision, of sailors, midshipmen, passed-mid-
shipmen, commanders, lieutenants, captains.
Above these in their order, he said, was the
commodore. Then they asked how many
grades were above a commodore. It was before
the times of admirals, and young MacDonald
told them of the Navy-Board, the Secretary
of the Navy, and the President.

" ' And who is above the President?' I told them," said he, " that the people was above the President. But of that they could make nothing."

" Of that they could make nothing?" No : of that they could make nothing. Men trained under a pure feudal system, of which the late Japanese government gave the finest illustration to our time, never can make any thing of this central principle. I do not remember any writer of note in England, in our time, who has succeeded in grasping this idea. The popular conception given in the English books is, that our system is an elective monarchy with fixed periods of reign. The analogy is constantly sought between the President of the nation, and the king of a kingdom. There is no analogy. The President is the servant of a sovereign. The king is a person, who, however selected, after he is selected, is the fountain of honor, and at least the arbiter between the leading subjects. The distinction between a citizen and a subject is equally wide. In the feudal or European systems, no man may do

any thing unless he is permitted. In the
democratic or American system, any man may
do any thing unless he is forbidden. The
difference is as great as that between starlight
and noon. In Germany, I may not live in a
town twenty-four hours without asking per-
mission of the police; I may not build a carriage
unless I have a permit as a carriage-builder; I
may not write a recipe unless I am licensed as
a physician; I may not tell you that you sung
*b* flat instead of *b* natural unless I am licensed
as a music-teacher; nay, I may not preach the
very gospel of good tidings unless I am licensed as a preacher. But in America I may
preach, if you will listen; and if you will not
listen, I may preach to the winds. I may build
as many coaches as I like, only if the wheels
are not round the people will not ride in them.
The function of oversight or command with
us is in the hands of the people, unorganized
and without form; while under those systems
of government it belongs to the political authorities.

From this it results that fully nine-tenths

of the functions of political government in the Old World are retained here by the people,— by the sovereign,—in his own hands. Only one-tenth, then, of the force, talent, or genius needed for political administration in the Old World is required here in the same service. Whole bureaux or departments of administration in the service of the Old World are unknown in our arrangement, and only one-tenth goes there. We need no department of worship, for the people administers the Church. We need, in most States, no department of the higher education: the people administers the colleges. Generally speaking, we need no department of commerce, or of agriculture. We need but a small military bureau, because the army is not one-twentieth part of the army of any other first-rate power. The people builds the railroads, the steamships, and orders the agricultural contests, the rewards, and inventions. Generally speaking, we need no department of fine arts or public amusements. The people builds the Museum, arranges the School of Art, crowns the painter or the sculptor. The people opens the Lyceum,

the Theatre, or the Opera, and the people closes
them.

What men choose still to call "the Government" or "the Administration" reduces itself
to what has a mere handful of attributes, if contrasted with what Government must claim in
absolute or in feudal systems. Let us not be
deceived by the accident of a name. Let us
not suppose that because we call the bureaux of
political administration "the Government," it
is only they who govern. And let us not make
the mistake of the Old World critics, of supposing that it is among them only that our
leaders are to be found.

II.   In simple society, the Leaders, of course,
come to the front, —

> "Of native impulse, elemental force."

It will be conceded, I believe, that this hap-
pened a hundred years ago, in the Revolutionary
times.  The land had no lack of leaders then:
that is conceded.  We are far enough away
from those times to see who they were.  They
appeared when they were wanted; and they

did what they had to do. They led; and, where
they led, men followed. All this is the easier
to see, because the pretenders — the men who
could not lead — are clean forgotten, as we look
back. Time teaches history well. Time shows
us the leaders; and we need not distress ourselves in looking for the failures.

And these leaders, whence came their commis-
sions? Samuel Adams, Washington, Franklin,
Greene, Morris, and a hundred others who led
this land as it needed to be led, — what brought
them forward? Ask, rather, what could have
kept them back? Is it any vote of an Assembly
that directs Samuel Adams to insist, through
and through, on Independence? Is it any hereditary right which puts him in a position to
maintain it? He has that word to speak: he
speaks, and men are compelled to hear. So of
Washington, so of Greene, the commanders of
your armies. No man will pretend that it needed
a commission from the Assembly of Virginia, or
from that of Rhode Island, to make those men
your leaders in successful wars. What changed
Henry Knox, the Boston bookseller, into the

engineer in command of your artillery?   What
so taught him that he

"Created all the stores of war"?

Had you to wait till such a man was born in
some predestined succession?   Or had you to
wait till he was trained to that service by a series of red-taped and decorous promotions?   Not
a bit of it!   You needed him, and you found
him.   Your lines of promotion were open, so
that nothing checked him.   For that purpose,
as the event proved, he was your leader: and
the leader led !

This is conceded, I say, for times of exigency,
of great trial.   "These are the days of miracle," men say.   The knot deserves solution,
and from the skies some god descends.   But
then they turn to peaceful times, and they claim
that the principle will not apply.   For instance
(and for this purpose it is a very striking instance), men urge the three administrations
of the Virginian dynasty of Presidents ; beginning with Jefferson, and running down,

"Fine by degrees, and miserably less,"

till it ends with James Monroe. Or, if you please to make a point even finer, you may taper it with the reign of John Tyler. And sceptics say to you, "Are these your leaders? Where did they lead you?" Well, it is true that, of the last two persons I have named, most men in this assembly perhaps would say nothing, — good, bad, or indifferent, — simply because men remember nothing about them and have nothing to say. Nay, it is true, I suppose, that Jefferson himself had made his last gift to the people of this land, when he had well announced the principle I am maintaining, — namely, that to the people as sovereign may well be entrusted, without intermediate delegation, by far the largest share of the people's own affairs. Grant then — what I suppose is true — that for four and twenty years at the beginning of this century, from 1801 to 1825, the so-called heads of this nation led it in no direction. Grant that neither of these three Presidents has proved in fact to be a leader. Grant that no principle for which they struggled has proved to be worth a straw, and that every measure for which they contended has proved to be a vanity. The one great event of Jefferson's reign, the acquisition of Louisiana, is no work of his policy. It was the suggestion and the work of no less a man than Napoleon Bonaparte.

"I have given England a rival," he said to Marbois, when he signed the act of cession.

All this is simply to grant that the chief servants of the people, in those four and twenty years, were not its leaders. Is that so strange? Are wise men often led by their servants? Were not the people led all the same? Why, in those very years, here was Eli Whitney leading them in the development of the new product, cotton, which gave to this little line of sea-board colonies (for they were still such) the great counterpoise in the necessary exchanges of the world. Here were such leaders as Hopkins, of Newport, and Emmons, of Franklin, at work in their Spartan studies, leading the speculation of the men of thought and of religion over the land, as they weighed out in their balances the very attributes of the Almighty. Here again was Robert Fulton leading it steadily forward, though the land did not know that it was led, by his persistency in his great invention, without which, indeed, that whole purchase of Louisiana was almost valueless, — an invention which, in its application there alone, called into existence half a continent, whose harvests this day feed half a world. Such men as Allston were leading the country to triumphs of art. Such men as Andrew Jackson were leading the Western pioneers, and teaching them the terrible might of this land for war. Such men as Channing were opening a new page before men's eyes as to the relations of man with God, and God with man ; were leading men

"Nearer, my God, to thee."

Could a land be better led? And who named these leaders? What commission did they need from this or that Board of returns? What herald's certificate did they need of their hereditary right to command? They led, because they were leaders. And where they led, men followed!

It is the custom of our time, — I am sorry to

say that it is the custom of occasions like this, —
to lament that the scholars and men of letters
of the country are not placed in places of political administration.    Has the history of the
country showed that it needed its first ability
at Washington?   Were such men as I have
named, — such men as Whitney and Fulton,
such men as Channing and Hopkins, — wasted
because they were not in the Senate or in the
Cabinet?   Take such a life as that of Francis
Wayland, who for a quarter of a century directed
the education of thousands of young men in
Brown University: will any one seriously say
that it would be better for this country to-day, if
he had spent those years in the Senate chamber
at Washington?   May I not ask, even in this
presence, without impropriety, whether such a
name as that of Mark Hopkins will not go
down to posterity with fresher laurels and with
more certainty of fame, because he has been the
foster-father of the pupils of this Alma Mater,
than it would have earned in any forensic struggles, or in any legislative arena?   Or, in one
word, is this people short-sighted?  Men are

apt to say that they are too shrewd. Does not
this people know where it most needs service?
And if we find that great men, unselfish men,
thoughtful men, and men of genius, — men of
a pure ambition, and of strong resolve, — do not
choose the career of administration for their
career, have we not reason to think that they
know the field of fame and the field of duty as
well as we do?

Let me adduce a single instance of a single
detail of administration, which has proved of
great importance. The system of the issues of
bank-notes in this country requires that their
amount shall be regulated by a deposit of government stocks, not held by the bank officers,
but placed in the hands of the public administration. This principle, first tried in New York
in 1838, was copied in many other States, and
borrowed by Sir Robert Peel in England, in
1844. It is now the basis of the National Bank
circulation of America. Who is the author of
it? The author was the President of Columbia
College, who proposed it in his lectures to his
seniors, and demonstrated its fitness. One of

those seniors afterwards introduced it into the legislation of New York. From the system of New York it passed into the legislation of the world. The improvement was needed, and it came. Can you suggest any possible system for the choice of your rulers, in which it should have come more easily?

III. It will happen, of course, that there come crises of importance, when the political administration is the pivot on which all interests turn, and the welfare of the country hinges. Wisdom, and the first wisdom; prudence, and the first prudence; courage God-born, — is then needed by the officers in that service. Never fear, when that moment comes, but that they will watch the people, and obey the Leaders of the people, whether the Leaders be in this office or in that, or in none; whether they wear this, that, or another crown of honor. What is Abraham Lincoln's great honor, but that he understood the instincts of the American people, knew what it wanted, what it meant, and what it would do? In point of fact, you find pessimism and despair among those persons who see least of the real people of this land. The men who see only the drunken class of foreigners in Boston, in New York and Chicago, may well be in doubt as to our political institutions. But you will notice that that doubt is never shared by the men who meet, whether on the stump or in daily converse, the freeholders of the Western States, — the men who have made their own houses, their own farms, their own schools, their own churches, their own laws. They know that such men will make their own officers, and will unmake them.

Yes, and more than this: those officers, when made, be the name President, Senator, Secretary, chief clerk, or under clerk; be he head of a bureau, or the lowest messenger boy of a porter, — those officers listen obediently, take to heart, digest, and obey the directions of the Leaders of the people, be those Leaders where they may. It is some unknown penman in his closet; it is some Lowell singing a song; it is some Emerson dreaming a dream; it is some Moody moving a multitude; it is some Tom

Scott annihilating time; it is some Sampson organizing emigration; it is some Phillips on a rostrum; or it is Mark Hopkins in this pulpit. The officer of the administration sits at the centre where a thousand mirrors reflect, where a thousand telephones repeat the words, and, like the obedient genie when Aladdin rubs his lamp, the officer of administration starts up, to say, —

"I HEAR, AND I OBEY."

IV.  Gentlemen, I will not leave this subject, addressing as I do the chosen representatives of so many of the most favored young men of the Northern States, without offering a word to them of practical suggestion.  Take it, in Alpha Delta Phi, as the counsel of an older brother.

In this business of the choice of a career, which occupies you already, you will defer to the last possible moment mere study for your specialty.  A specialty there must be at last, but put off as long as you may your special preparation.  Distrust all charlatans who tell you that they have a patent process to fit you for any one career in life, — whether they call it a Commercial College, a Normal School, or a double-combination-refined Elective, — without broad Liberal Culture as the basis. Do not listen to the man who advises you to go into the business of making weather-cocks and steeples for churches, without building towers, and walls, and strong crypts, and foundations underground.

Then, when the profession is chosen, and prepared for, consecrate yourself to God as his servant in it, that its work shall be done well. " Be ye perfect, even as your Father who is in heaven is perfect." That is the rule. Whether you open a copper mine in Michigan ; whether you plough and sow and harvest a thousand acres in Illinois; whether you organize labor, and make cosmos out of chaos in Louisiana; whether you preach the gospel of Christ in some lonely village in the mountains ; whether you wait for clients who will not come, but prepare, while you are waiting, to unravel the knot of Gordius himself, — whatever you do, do that work well. Do it as a Leader does it.

2

This country has founded these colleges, it has endowed these professorships, it has selected you to be students, that you may be its educated leaders. Gentlemen, do not be false to her! Lead you will, if lead you can. See that you are leaders, by doing well what you have to do.

I do not say that you are to avoid what is called Public Life. I say you are to enter one of its duties or another, as it may happen. For the truth is that you are in it, of course, if you do your duty. Men, trained as you are, speak easily when you have any thing to say. God forbid that else you should speak at all! Men, trained as you are, write simply what you have to teach. It is your fault then, so far, if the Press, where you live, falters, or does not say what it might do. A free press, and an open rostrum, is the privilege of course of every educated American gentleman. Whoever else in this world complains that he cannot move men as he should, it is not men to whom are open avenues like these.

Do well what you do. And do it conscious

that you ought to be Leaders among men. It is said to be the privilege of the young American that he may be what Miltiades was, and Alcibiades, — a founder of a State, if he choose. Gentlemen, this founding of a State does not require us to cross the mountains. Wherever our lot is thrown, we may dig deep for the foundations, and build solidly the walls of the institutions which are to stand. And whether our names perish or are remembered, such institutions, in the days that are to come, will be the monuments to those who come after us, that these men builded well!

And, above all, do not blow your own trumpets; nor, which is the same thing, ask other people to blow them. No trumpeter ever rose to be a general. If the power to lead is in you, other men will follow. If it is not in you, nothing will make them follow. It is for you to find the eternal law of this universe, and to put yourself in harmony with that law. Speaking more simply, it is to find God, and to work as fellow-laborer with Him. Do that, and you may afford to be indifferent, who else works with you.

" Self-reverence, self-knowledge, self-control :
   These three alone lead men to sovereign power !
   Yet not for power : power of itself would come
   Uncalled for.   But to live by law,
   Acting the law we live by, without fear ;
   And, because right is right, to follow right, —
   Were wisdom in the spite of consequence."

## II.

## THE SPECIALTIES.

JOHN MILTON returned to England, from his foreign travels, just as England was on the edge of civil war. In France and in Italy he had been welcomed with enthusiasm. He had been fairly petted by scholars; he had been jealously watched by cat-like inquisitors, afraid that he was budding heresies into the true vine; he had been serenaded by musicians; he had been sung by poets; he had been beloved by all. But Milton would not stay to be petted or flattered. The thunders growled in the horizon of England; the batteries were builded which were to open on the English Sumter; and the true Englishman knew, the true Christian knew, that in such an exigency his place was home. He left sunny Italy for foggy London; left flattery to find abuse; left play for work, and work the hardest. He had been graduated at the uni-

versity a few years before. I may say that,
when he turned his back upon Italy, his last
vacation was over, and the real commencement
of his life had come.

I may, then, fairly allude to his life as an
illustration for some inquiries which we will
make as to liberal study, such as that to which
the readers of this book devote themselves.
Here is the man on the whole most distinguished
among men of our race, if, in our estimate of
distinction, we are to give a fair estimate to personal purity, to moral greatness, and to intellectual power.  Of all men who have spoken
our language, Shakspeare and Milton are the
two whose loss, if we can conceive of it, would
be the most fatal; and, of these two, John
Milton is the man who, in thought and action,
in character, in politics, in his hope and effort
for the coming-in of the kingdom of heaven, —
say, in one word, in his religion, — represents
the idea and the prophecy most dear to America,
and especially to young America.  Some illustrations drawn from that master life ought to be
of use to young America to-day.

John Milton was the first scholar of his time;
he was the first theologian of his time; he was
the first statesman of his time; he was the first
poet of his time.

He was the first scholar of his time. When
Charles the Second, fleeing into exile, wished to
establish his cause before Europe, he retained
the person then accredited as the first man of
letters in Europe, Claude de Saumaise, to write
out the justification of Charles I., his father.
At the order of the Parliament, Milton replied.
He rode over Saumaise in their tournament, as
Charlemagne or Roland would have ridden down
and ridden over Don Quixote. And the name
of the showy scholar, who knew, men said, every
thing worth knowing, exists to-day in the dreariest corner of the dreariest cyclopædia, only
because Milton honored him with a reply.

Milton was the first theologian of his time.
Not even his friends who made the Westminster
Confession; not even such sweet spirits as Her-
bert and Vaughan and Chillingworth and Taylor,
who in an opposing camp showed their unity of
the spirit with those who overthrew the crown

and the throne ; not Hooker, Baxter, and Law ; nor, on our side the water, not any Cotton or Davenport or Mather or Williams of them all, — have so held the faith of the world, have so swayed its devotion or so guided its prayer, as he who invoked the Holy Spirit for his muse, and taught all men the music of the first evening hymn.

Looking back upon it all, we have a right to say he was the first statesman of his time. Cromwell and the rest were trained in that rough school of statesmanship which does not miss its mark. Like our own dear Abraham Lincoln, when the common sense of the people pushed them on, they found out how to lead. There was no lack of will, and they found out the way. But when they had to defend in letters the work that they had done ; when, as against a defeated church, or a throne overturned, they had to justify in eternal argument their cause, — whom had they to turn to but John Milton?

That he was the first poet of his time, the world allows. There are not wanting those who say he was the first poet of all time.

Now, what was the training which stood Milton in stead for service so various to the world? What were the early studies which laid the foundation for work so distinguished, — work in lines so different, which was, however, work so bravely, nay, so completely done? There are ugly proverbs which say that a "Jack at all trades works ill at all." That may be true of trades: clearly it is not true of the nobler range of service. How was Milton trained in boyhood and in youth, that, when a man, he might serve his country and his God, whether as advocate, whether as theologian, whether as statesman or as poet? The answer is in familiar words. As boy and youth, thanks to a fond father's wisdom, Milton had the most generous, the broadest culture England or Europe had to give. He enjoyed what we rightly call a liberal education.

The world was then what it is now, in the habit of men's minds and in the drift of their ambitions. There is no doubt, therefore, that John Milton and his father were surrounded with people who advised some other training. They urged, I do not doubt, what people now call a specialty; that this young man should be early trained to some special pursuit, trade, or calling. As time passed on, I do not doubt that they pointed out the success, the brilliant success, of this or that specialist, as illustrative of the value of their counsel. The chief contractor who made Cromwell's powder, for instance (there must have been such a man, though history has forgotten him), — the master manufacturer who made the powder which Cromwell's soldiers kept so dry, and burned to so much purpose, — was, doubtless, in the London of that day, a person of more mark and note than John Milton. He had wrought on his specialty, and had wrought on it well. He had made a good contract, he made good powder, and he got good pay. History has forgotten him; but I dare reconstruct history so far as to say that I am sure he rode in his carriage, while Milton went afoot; that his wife had laces and silks fit for an empress, while Milton's wife spread thin butter on thick bread for hungry schoolboys. I think the powder-contractor and the poet may have known each other at school. I think he may have nodded good-naturedly to Milton, as they met some day at the government offices; and I can hear the contractor saying to himself, with contemptuous pity; "That is what comes of the classics and the mathematics, Christ College and the university; and my coach and four here are what came of my specialty." Yet, for all that, if we had to choose between the two lines for son of ours, we should not choose the special training; we should choose the liberal education. For we should say: "It is perfectly certain that the powder manufacturing will be done; it is not perfectly certain that, without watchful care and delicate nursing, the world will get its science, its statesmanship, its theology, or its poetry." About the methods in life there need be no fear. The doubt and danger are about the principles on which all methods depend. The methods of life are all that the specialist fully learns. The man of liberal education is studying its principles.

It is unquestionably true that, with the immense enlargement of human knowledge, the several sciences part so widely that no man can pretend to master them all; and only the merest charlatan professes the knowledge of the detail of every vocation. Still it is as true as ever, first, that all science involves a knowledge of fundamental and essential principles, and that the man who is not trained and habituated in these will be a mere dabster and empiric, even in the method of the special science which he has chosen. It is true, again, that each science is to be investigated and explained by the same eternal laws of truth and methods of reasoning as every other; and the specialist who undertakes to study or to teach without habit and experience in these laws of truth and methods of reasoning, breaks down again as dabster and pretender. Once more, it is true that, as the unity of Nature asserts itself, and the correlation of one force with another, that man succeeds best in interpreting Nature in one of her phases who can best interpret her in another. This is the man who, from the breadth of his education, can tell something of the harmony of things, of the cosmos of the universe. He succeeds in his specialty just in proportion to the breadth of his general education.

Yet it is necessary to say this, and to illustrate it by such memories as those which tell us to what education we owe John Milton, and how great the loss would have been had we specialized him into a scrivener; because, in the rush of our time, even the colleges and universities have been invaded, and the old narrowness of the specialty is here and there proclaimed anew, as if it were some new discovery in education.

When we come to examine this tempting and specious proposal, does it amount to any thing more than the old temptation, that the child of God shall use the heavenly power God has given him by setting it to make bread out of stones?

What do we say of the same proposal when it is presented a little earlier in men's lives?

In my own home, the city of Boston, there is an annual expenditure for the education of children of about a million and a half of dollars. The poorest child may take the advantage of this expenditure till he is eighteen years of age; and the methods are so arranged that he may, if he choose, enter with good instruction on many of the lines of study pursued in most colleges. In spite of this generous provision, however, the larger part of the children leave school before they are twelve years old. They do this that they may acquire certain specialties. It is now the specialty of selling lozenges, or matches; it is now the specialty of leasing opera-glasses for the evening; it is now the specialty of what is called a cash-boy in a large retail store. It is not an apprenticeship, which educates a boy for higher life: at twelve, he is too young for that. It is only a specialty which enables him to earn, week by week, about as much as will pay for his food.

When we see this in the case of the little boy or girl, we all regret it. There is then no question that the decision of the parents is wrong. By all means in our hands we attempt to change that decision. In Boston, we are at this moment trying to introduce into the school system such technical education in sewing, in carpentry, and other useful arts, as may persuade short-sighted parents to keep their children at school a little longer; for we think even half a loaf is better than no bread. We do not do this because we like to do it: we accept it as the necessity forced upon us by the determination of ignorant parents to gain the immediate return of bread and butter for the education which is given to their children. We see that the longer we can put off the acquisition of the specialty, the better.

This principle, which is acknowledged by all in the case of boys and girls, loses none of its force when it is applied in the lives of young men and young women. Of course, in civilized life, each man, sooner or later, must have his special training in the service which he is to render. But the precise object for which we have founded colleges is to give the liberal and broad foundation on which that training is to be based. And the rule of life might be stated, almost without an exception, that the longer the special training could be postponed, so the generous preparation were still in progress, the better for the man, and the better for mankind.

The fine and analytic division of labor for

which the specialist pleads, results, he thinks,
in a certain improvement in the quantity or the
quality of the world's manufacture. If one
man always does one thing, and another man
always does another thing, each man growing
perfect in his specialty, the result will be, we
are told, better pins in your pin-factory, more
sheetings from your majestic mills, finer type
for your newspapers, and Remington rifles more
highly finished in your armories. All this is
very possible. But the argument forgets that
this world was not created for the manufacture
of pins, of sheetings, of newspapers, or of rifles:
it was created for the training of men. And
the man is made more perfect and more, not by
his deftness in this handicraft, or his knack in
that trade ; but as one part of his being is thoroughly wrought in with another part, body with
mind, and mind with soul.

The great modern patron of that system of
industry which makes each man do what he can
do cheapest, and divides labor so that one man
shall make the heads of pins perfectly, and shall
be capable of nothing else; that another man

shall point them perfectly, and be fit for nothing else, — is Adam Smith. It might be enough to say that, if Adam Smith's theory could have been properly carried out, he would have spent his life, not in writing treatises of political economy, but in fishing for herrings on the shore of Scotland: that being the industry for which Nature seems to have best fitted that region, had not the restrictions of government or civilization introduced other life there. Adam Smith is himself, then, an illustration how much the world gains when the boy or the man is trained to some broader and higher life than the mere specialty to which circumstances, or what people call "nature," would have directed him. Have we not, in our own history, had instances, — instances enough, to teach us what the country gains by training its citizens in the broader culture? Like the old Greek culture, it enables them to turn to any service. What is the whole tenor of the history of the war? Who were our diplomatists, — our Adams, and Marsh, and Motley? They were men who had been trained in the broader culture, and took up the specialty

of diplomacy as a matter of course, just as
Themistocles led a fleet without having been
trained to the specialty of a sailor.  The special
accomplishment, indeed, is only charlatanism,
when it is not based on knowledge of the principle employed.  Such is the rule-of-thumb
reckoning of the seaman who does not know
why his latitudes and longitudes come right,
and is wholly the slave of his process.

It was my fortune, once, to sit for several
days by the side of the late Governor Andrew,
of Massachusetts, while, with skill and success
which I will not pretend to describe, he presided
over a large, excited assembly, which, but for
his admirable gift, would have been stormy.
When all was done, I ventured to felicitate him
on his success.  "I think I have succeeded," said
he; "and I believe it is because, in all my life,
I have only for three or four hours been in the
chair of any assembly.  I believe it is because
I know nothing of the technics of parliamentary
law.  I mean," he added, with earnestness,
"that I have been trying all through these days
to apply the principles of justice, of truth, and

common sense, in the forms, which were of course familiar to me, of deliberative assemblies." I could not but contrast that verdict with the verdict of my distinguished kinsman, John P. Hale, who stood with me one day, in the gallery at the Capitol, as an acute parliamentarian,—who has thus far never been any thing but an acute parliamentarian,—dissected some point of order to the bottom. " I would not," said Mr. Hale, "know as much as that man knows of parliamentary law,—no, not if you gave me the world!" Take that as a not unfair contrast of the difference between principle and method, if, by any misfortune, either must be learned alone.

The man who does not understand the principle will constantly be blundering in his method. The amusing stories of the blunders of the accurate Chinese imitators are illustrations. But more than this, and worse than this, the specialist who has not laid a generous foundation for his art cannot explain it to another; cannot wisely conduct the experiments for advancing it: he can only repeat the processes to which he himself is bred. The hackneyed anecdote says that Mansfield told the Indian judge, who had not been trained in the principles of law, to make his decisions boldly, and they would be right; but to beware how he gave his reasons, for they would surely be wrong. Precisely so: the mere specialist cannot give his reasons. He has to work by a recipe; and what becomes of such work? It was such work which the artisans of old time wrought in, — in the lost arts, — over whose monuments we are left to wonder. Such workmen learned the process, but they were powerless to explain the principle; so the abiding or eternal element was gone. The science ceased to be a science: it became an art, a knack, a secret, a memory, a shadow, — and then was gone for ever.

Of modern science, on the other hand, the glory is, that it is built up on certain eternal principles which have found their formulas in what we call laws. A knowledge of these laws leads to the true experiment, and to the simplifying of science. All true science is seeking to make science simpler and simpler: it is seeking to find the general principle of which these special arts are only the illustrations. The greatest victory of modern science — the correlation of physical forces — is an exquisite instance of the answer given to men who were able to interrogate Nature, not with one but with many questions. And the bold suggestions and fascinating generalizations of the most distinguished naturalists of our time, — of the Darwins and Huxleys and Tyndalls, — are gifts to us from minds which have been trained, not in one line of research, nor in two, but in many: I might almost say in all. Their generalization takes its value from the range of their observation. Then the statement of it is intelligible, because they have not disregarded intellectual sciences of analysis, of investigation, and of argument. And, once more, their methods are intelligible because there is, and they know there is, a principle behind.

The truth seems to be that, for all these reasons, we should be glad in every case to postpone the training for the specialty as long as possible. We are to make the studies in preparation for it broad enough to train every faculty of body, mind, or soul. It is only in the lowest grades of life that we do not find fault with the absence of either side of such training. We do not expect, perhaps, that a hod-carrier shall move gracefully, or speak fluently, or talk without profanity. But just so soon as life calls for leaders, just so soon as a crisis comes, so soon as education, or men of education, are in question, — we ask that body, mind, and soul, all shall be quite ready for our service.

Does any one venture to make what men call the crucial test the test of success in war? If you inquire there, our own experience is all on one side. The education of West Point, which has given such vigor to our armies, is thoroughly liberal, and by no means technical or special. What men write English like your West Point army officers? What men better understand the relations of science with science? Nay, what men have been more successful in their practical interpretation of constitutional law? And if you will ask the most successful of them as to what is the best preparation for West

Point, they will tell you, without exception, that the best introduction to West Point is the full training of one of our colleges. And if you look outside West Point, in the army, the verdict is the same. What men rose to rank most distinguished, and won the love as well as the honors of the country, as did the men whom the colleges had trained, not for one service only, but to be ready for whatever call of duty? Let me indulge a personal regard, and speak with a regret which is not personal but national, in naming for my own *Alma Mater* our Lowell and Wadsworth. Or let me speak for the country when I name men still living, — Hayes and Terry, and Butler and Chamberlain, and Hawley and Howard. Did not such men lead their soldiers under fire more cheerfully, because every memory of old heroism and storied victory was theirs, — the memories of Mantinea and Thermopylæ and Lutzen and Naseby? Did they not care for their soldiers more tenderly because their eyes had overflowed when they read of the gentle ministries of St. Louis and St. Vincent? Did not they rule conquered cities more firmly

and more wisely because they had early learned
how to love a Curtius and to scorn a Verres?
Nay, such men died more easily, the eye of the
body closed with one smile more tender creeping
over the cold features, because, as they died,
they remembered what Harvard and Yale and
Brunswick and Lewiston and Dartmouth had
taught them in their boyhood: "Blessing and
honor indeed, that a man may die for his country!"

But I do not choose to discuss these questions on the strength of any illustrations, however pertinent or strong. I am addressing
young men whose lives are consecrated to
liberal study, in colleges founded for liberal
study, or preparing for them. No college can
pretend to liberal study unless it is baptized
in the free thought of its founders. Addressing
them, I need only refer to the central demand
of all Christian education, — the demand made
by him who was a scholar before he was an
apostle; who, in the schools of Jewish thought,
and even from the teachers of Gentile wisdom,
had learned what the wisdom of men had to say

in these things. It is St. Paul who rises above the wisdom of the flesh to speak to you in the words of the Spirit. It is Saint Paul who says, in words which might be well taken for the eternal motto of a new-born college, that the aim of all life, the object of all training, is that we may come unto a perfect man: εἰς ἄνδρα τελείον, — "Unto a perfect man!"

It is not simply the training of the voice to speak; it is not simply the training of the eye to see; far less is it the training of the fingers of the hand to this service or that toil. It is that we may come unto a perfect man. The whole body, soul and spirit, are to be presented blameless, — the body, by those exercises and by that temperance which come from the wisdom that is first pure; the mind, by that discipline which shall quicken fancy, shall strengthen memory, and shall clear argument from sophistry. And the soul, the infinite child of an infinite God, is to be trained in faith and hope and love: in faith to look above the world; in hope to look beyond time; in love to look outside its lesser life, in that communion in which we are one with all God's children, one even with himself. This is the standard, which the great Christian apostle proposes for your education. Try his experiment, and look forward to nothing less than this ultimate blessing. Then let life offer what it may; let the special duty be here or there; let the hand be called for, or the head, or the heart; let it be words of conviction, or deeds of valor, or prayers of faith, which the world needs, — we are equipped for the one call or the other. We stand not hampered by the little habits of some petty training; we stand forth ready, — ay, ready, the willing sons of Almighty God, strong in the liberty in which Christ has made us free.

## III.

## NOBLESSE OBLIGE.

An Address delivered before the Annual Convention
of Alpha Delta Phi, May 18, 1871.

NEARLY twenty of the chief colleges of America assemble here to-day. The vision of a far-sighted man, who thought it possible to unite the educated men of America in a certain unseen tie of friendship, is so far accomplished. The fittest solemnities of such an occasion would be, perhaps, a generous rivalry of letters between the institutions represented. As Yale and Harvard, Amherst and Brown, meet at Lake Quinsigamond to test muscle and endurance on the water, what if *A. Δ. Φ.* should institute such games as those in which Herodotus and Pindar won victories in the days of laurels? — if here, not one orator spoke alone, nor one poet sang, but if from every *Alma Mater* there were a lyric; or if he

who had composed a history first published it
to the world by reading here a chapter, and if
we awarded to the fittest the first wreath of the
crowns of thirty centuries?   Well, if from one
Sybaris or another, it prove that one Herodotus
or another among you, gentlemen, have this
chapter of history in his pocket, or if one Pindar or another is ready to sing his lay, my
friend the poet, and I, the more prosaic spokes-
man, will not delay them long.   It is ours to
introduce the feast of learning, which, if we
adopt that custom of the Alpha Deltas of the
Isthmus, will continue, I think, for many days.
I will be satisfied, in such preface, to speak only
as one of so many representatives of the seats
of learning.   I will not pretend that we are all
scholars.   At the bottom of our hearts we know
that none of us deserve that name.   But I will
speak to men of the liberal professions, as one
who has had a liberal education.   To education
in the liberal arts, in the humanities, our colleges are pledged and our fraternity is consecrated.   By education to the humanities, and
in the liberal arts, our lives have been blessed,

we are the men we are, and we enjoy what we
enjoy. In daily life we may be hewers of wood
and drawers of water; but we hew and we
draw with a certain divine energy, and can
make the humblest duty shine. Nay: this also
is true, that from the moment when we elected
liberal study for our study, the liberal arts for
our arts, the liberal professions for our callings,
— the whole community combined to help us
on. For us it has endowed its Yale and its
Cornell. For us it has founded the Astor
Library and the Franklin Academy. For us
it established in every new State marked out
upon the map in the wilderness such a foundation for a university as no emperor of
them all ever gives to letters. We then, as
men of the liberal professions or as those who
look forward to them, consider, almost of
course, when we meet together, what are the
essential attributes of these professions, and
what we owe, in every-day life, to Church and
State, which have vied with each other in es-
tablishing them and maintaining them.

*Noblesse Oblige!* — Our privilege compels us!

This was the battle-cry with which the Duke
de Levis, one of the old *régime* of France, tried
to quicken the new *noblesse*, created by Napoleon, and to point them their duty in the State.
The French dictionaries of to-day will tell you
that it is an " old proverb." The idea is as
old and as new as the word of Him who said,
he " who is greatest among you shall be your
servant." But this was not an idea believed
in by the old *noblesse* of France. And its
revival in new expression, when Napoleon tried
to renew that nobility, marks well enough the
period in modern history, when the world was
becoming so far Christian that men of great
opportunities were all taught that they had
great responsibilities. The Count Laborde is
my authority for saying that this noble Christian axiom is in form thus modern.

The old *noblesse* of France never made public
expression of the idea. But the motto illustrates fairly enough the responsibility which,
in all countries and in all times, is on the leaders of the people. In our country, in our time,
it is the responsibility which rests on the men

of liberal culture and of the liberal professions.
Public spirit, which is the life-breath of the
Commonwealth; *publicus spiritus*, the breath
which, if it cannot draw, it is stifled and dies;
public spirit, which colors red the lazy life-
blood of the State, gives it its oxygen, gives
it quickness, gives it victory, — public spirit
will so quicken it, if we do our duty, speak our
word, put our shoulders to the wheel. If we
fail, that public spirit pants heavily and slowly.
For the men of liberal culture, of the liberal
arts and professions, — for the men who have
had such advantage as the training of the
higher humanities attempts to give, — I say all
these advantages demand of us special sacrifices
in the public service; that we quicken as we
can the public life; that we live as we may in
a public spirit. *Noblesse Oblige!* Each gift
that the past has given to us is pledge for our
discharge of the common duty.

I. If I had no other reason for saying this, I
should be tempted to make it the subject of my
address to-day, because of the habit bred among

persons who do not know what liberal culture
is, of reducing all art, study, philosophy, and
religion to what the Germans call bread-and-
butter vocations. When the Saviour of mankind entered upon his work among men, the
arch-tempter of mankind tried the first of dev-
ilish wiles upon him, by trying to persuade him
to debase the life divine by some selfish miracle
which should make bread for his own personal
hunger. The same tempter offers the same
temptation to each child of God this day. And
in the several voices by which the Father of lies
addresses men, he tries to make them believe
that according as they succeed in coining the
divine gift, or in exchanging it for bread, or
palace, or fine clothing, or other personal luxury, in that proportion have their lives succeeded. Thus they will tell you that Demas
has made a good thing of it because he sold his
article in the " Review " for two hundred and
fifty dollars. Thing, indeed! They will tell
you that such or such a clergyman preached so
many sermons in a year, and that the treasurer
of his church paid him such or such a salary ;

that, therefore, each sermon was worth so many dollars, so many cents, so many mills, and so many infinitesimal fractions. They will tell you that the charming little bas-relief by Green-ough, in whose simple composition lingers a prayer — only not spoken in words — which for century upon century will lift spirits eternal nearer heaven, sold for only five hundred dollars; while the piled-up bronze of some Alexander the copper-smith, which insults high heaven in its angles, shocks low earth even in its tawdriness, and is destined to be cast into bell-metal as soon as the Right shall triumph in any happy revolution, — they will tell you that this piled-up hideousness cost half a million dollars, and is therefore a work of art of a thousand times the value of the other. By such absurd and forced analogies, all borrowed from the world of hogsheads and tierces and tons and quintals, do men degrade the aspira-tions and the victories of the only life that is life! Now, because this vulgar talk creeps into the journals and into general society, it seems fit to present the true purpose and motive of

3*

the liberal professions and the liberal arts, in a meeting of men who are pledged to them. We are not hirelings in our service. *Noblesse Oblige!* The very privileges which are conferred upon us compel us to do our duty. The endowments of the colleges, — every luxury of letters, — this freemasonry which makes us friends here, though we never saw each other's faces; every privilege of our lives as men of liberal training, — involves duties to the State and to mankind.

II. What, then, are the distinctions between a guild of craftsmen and a guild of men of liberal training? What account is to be given of the distinctions which we enjoy, as men of liberal culture, and which we know that we enjoy? The mock-modesty which pretends there are no such distinctions is but folly.

I do not speak first of the principle involved. Before we examine that, we shall notice two external and visible distinctions.

*First*, The liberal professions admit no secrets in their methods.

*Second*, In these professions, the compensation rendered is not computed with any relation to the service performed.

The historical distinction first to be noticed is that the professor, or the master of liberal arts, by whatever name he may be called, mediæval or of our own time, has no secrets in his calling. I suppose, if we cared to trace the history of language, we should find in this distinction alone the origin of the word "liberal" as applied to the freedom of art, — of science, — or, in general, of vocation.

Thus the great distinction of the artists to whom we owe the new birth of fine art in the middle ages is in the loyalty with which they taught all they knew. To surround himself with a staff of young and brilliant pupils, to work with them, to show them every process, to talk with them of every inspiration, nay, to intrust to their hands the execution of detail upon the canvas, — this was the method of the enthusiasm of the great Italian artists. It was thus that Raphael studied with Perugino; that Perugino, Leonardo, and Michel Angelo, at

one time or at another, studied together; that
Michel Angelo learned from Ghirlandaio.
Vasari says of Raphael that he never refused
to any artist, though he were wholly unknown
to him, his personal assistance in design or in
execution of any work; and in his studio he
was sometimes surrounded by fifty students,
some of them the most distinguished men of
his time, to whom he was glad indeed to teach
all he knew.

In every generation of such communion and
inspiration, by the divine law of selection itself,
Art gains something. "Nature gives us more
than all she ever takes away." The mere suggestion of the man of genius is worked out by
the care and sympathy of the man of talent; or
the ingenious plan and structure of the man of
talent is taken in hand and made effective by
the perseverance and adaptations of the man
of practice. Nay, let us not forget, in such
a review, the place filled by the mere drudge,
who thought he could only grind the color, or
rub down the surface, or hew the wood, or draw
the water for the more favored children of Art

in their divine imagining; for, as he faithfully does the duty that comes next his hand, how often has it proved that he also contributed what was essential to the whole: nay, how often has it been seen that here was the completer life, because of the slower development, and that when its hour of bud and blossom and perfume came, there unfolded from our unsightly cactus a wealth of crystalline color, spicy fragrance, and delicate grace which exceeded all the glories of precocious gardening! Such are the triumphs of Art, where the artist proves himself the true artist by taking all who come into his confidence, by keeping nothing secret which God has taught to him, but teaching freely to all who will hear all he knows he knows.

Perhaps it is easier for a clergyman to make this statement in its principle, because every one grants at once that in those cases, rare if you please, where our services are of any value, they are invaluable and beyond all price. A sermon of Robertson's, if it be of any use at all, is of transcendent and infinite value. The advice

which the country parson gave your brother
when he went away to sea, if it had any worth
at all, had worth not to be measured by any
human coinage. What, indeed, shall a man
give in exchange for his soul, if he have a soul?
St. Paul, therefore, the first of preachers, puts
this matter on a perfect basis in the very beginning, when he says that the man who gives his
life to the preaching of the gospel, or to other
ministry, is entitled somewhere and somehow to
a physical livelihood at the hands of the world
he serves. As to where or how the somewhere
or somehow comes, St. Paul is indifferent: let
the world settle that for itself. So he sends the
Epistle to the Philippians without entering it
for copyright at the clerk's office in the library
of the Senate; and he sends out the devil from
the possessed girl, in the streets of Philippi,
without asking her, as Dr. This or That whom
you or I could name would do, how much money
she is willing to pay in advance on the chances
of a cure. Not because Paul said it, but because it is essential common sense, this is the
necessary law of compensation for those callings

which deal with life, — life being in itself infinite and priceless. Nobody pays us for this special duty or that duty. The world is bound in general to see that we live. And there is no asceticism about this, nor what people call communism. The world must see that its servants so live as to render the most efficient service.

True, the world's servant must prove to the world that he can serve it. The world must compensate him at its estimate, and not at his own. But, beyond this, the particular method in which society or the world arranges for his compensation is matter, not of principle, but of detail. It will be settled by custom, or settled by history, or settled as a natural outgrowth of the organization of the country. The life-salary of a physician may be adjusted for him by the table of fees which the county medical society agree upon. I think very likely that may be the most convenient way. But he might be paid as a ship's surgeon is paid, by an annual salary; or he might be paid as they say the Chinese physicians are paid, a fixed income proportioned on the families in health in his dis-

trict, subject to a regular deduction, to be paid
by the doctors in pensions to those families
where there is disease.    Just so in a clergyman's
duty : his living may be secured to him by a tax
upon the land, as in England ; by a salary from
the government, as in France ; by alms collected
by begging, as with the Dominicans ; by a stated
annual compensation guaranteed by a particular
parish, as is sometimes the practice here ; or by
the varying contributions of the worshippers, as
is the custom sometimes.    The method is mere
leather and prunella : the essential is, that the
servant of the community in a liberal profession,
because he deals with infinite values, is entitled
to his living at the hands of the world he serves.
What follows is, that the world's servant in a
liberal profession renders his service without
stint or stop, to the full and utmost of his capacity.    Ready? ay, ready!    Body, mind, and
soul held ready for the noblest duty.    Never
overstrained, never sluggish, never fevered,
never torpid, never despondent, never extravagant, — all  this because never bought and
never sold !

The clergy and the doctors deal directly with life in distinct issues ; so that these illustrations seem most simple, perhaps, in the cases which I have cited. Life, being an infinite principle, is of infinite value. It is invaluable. But the principle is the same in all the liberal callings, for the reason that they all deal with infinite values, not to be weighed, counted, or measured. Such are the dealings of an artist : beauty in the finished marble, or on the glowing canvas, is of infinite value or it is of none. When we read " Viri Romæ " at school, we were taught to laugh at the barbarous consul who, when the statues of Corinth were packed for his Roman triumph, told the expressmen of that day that if they were broken they must make him new ones. But the same absurdity shows itself at Washington, whenever Congress limits an appropriation for a work of art, by saying it shall be made from American marble, or by an American artist, or perhaps by an artist who has never learned how, in order to give him an opportunity. I want my statue first-rate, or I do not want any ! Give me a fresh egg, or give me none at all !

So in education. Let tutor or professor give himself completely to his work, — body, soul, and spirit, — and I do not care whether he teaches my boy botany or electricity. The living soul will quicken other life. But let him give only the fag-end, the drainings, what there is left in the yellow sheets of the lectures of some other generation, again; he may lecture of Sanskrit or of Pleiocene to the boy, it is all one, — the one lecture is as useless as the other. Let him give his best, or let him give nothing.

I need no better illustration than the contrast between the free sports of your own ball-grounds and the prostituted exercise, purchased and paid for, of what is miscalled " professional ball-playing." The true aspirant in the liberal callings enters on his career as freshly and as bravely as you, young gentlemen, strike the ball, catch it, make a base, or wait your turn ; but the other has, of his own free will, degraded himself to the level of the so-called " professional club-man," who must throw so far or must strike so true or run so fast, or he has not earned his share in the day's receipts, and may lose his engagements for the next quarter!

I hope the American lawyer understands the
same truth, that, unless he deals with infinite
values, his profession is a handicraft and his
duty a job. Unless he deals with justice, pure
as heaven, — unless he deals with truth, virgin
as truth was born, — there is for him no ermine.
These States, in our organization of society,
have given distinguished position to the men of
his calling; have shielded them by privilege else
wholly unknown. They are exempt from many
of the burdens of other life, and see open to
them its highest honors. This is because they
are pledged in their very training, and by their
oaths of office are sworn, to obtain justice for all
men and for the State. The American lawyer
ought not to forget the traditions of his profession. The Templars of England, through
whose hands come down to him the methods of
the past, are the direct descendants of templars
bound to the service of chivalry. The only fee
which he receives is in form an "*honorarium*,"
— not the pay for service. The service is the
unbought service of the King of truth and of
right. He goes forth on his circuit, such is the

theory of his profession, with the same determination to protect the right and to crush the
wrong which sent out Launcelot or Arthur.
Who needs his help? Is it this poor boy, ar-
raigned for murder by a mad mob, because he
is of another color than theirs, and they will
wreak on him the wrath of centuries? Or is it
some child of luxury, born in the purple, who
has smiles and honors and gold for her minions?
He does his best, be it for the one or for the
other: ferrets out conspiracy; seizes truth,
though truth be hiding her face in tears ; and
compels the tribunal to decide rightly! The
moment that the American lawyer abandons
this position ; the moment that he sells justice,
or the share of justice that his services can command, to the highest bidder ; the moment he
says that the ring which can spend millions shall
have millions' worth, while the beggar with
a penny shall have a penny's worth, — in such
words of blasphemy he shows he has no knowledge of what justice is. He abandons the position of one who deals with infinite realities.
He has left, as one unfit, the ranks of a liberal

calling. He makes himself a mere craftsman, dealing with things alone, and to be recompensed with things alone. Leave him, gentlemen ; leave him to the company he deserves !

III. The visible distinctions, then, between the liberal professions and the crafts, or trades, are these two : —

*First*, That the liberal professions have, and can have, no secrets in their methods.

*Second*, That men engaged in them are not paid, and cannot be paid, piecemeal for their endeavors.

Woe to the doctor who does not his best for the poorest beggar as for the richest prince !

Woe to the clergyman who has fewer ministries of comfort for Lazarus than for Dives !

Woe to the lawyer who is other than the defender of ignorance against cunning !

Woe to the artist who carves less than his best in the marble, or paints other than his truest on the canvas !

Woe to the teacher who teaches by rote and catechism, and does not make the classic burn again with Virgil's fire, or the hard equation speak with the eloquence of truth divine!

And these two distinctions are enough to show that the essential principle which lifts the liberal professions to their place above all other callings, is that they deal directly with infinite values. They deal with infinite life, or life in one of its infinite relations. The callings of the teacher, the artist, the lawyer, the doctor, the clergyman, all assert their dignity because of this infinite element appearing directly in their endeavors. Can any other calling make the same claim? That moment there is another liberal profession, so long as that claim is true.

This, gentlemen of the Alpha Delta Phi, is the life for which your training in these universities is fitting you. In one ministry or another to which you are to devote yourselves, you are to be engaged in these highest of relations. Justice, Beauty, Truth, Life: it is to these that you consecrate your being,— to a chivalry, to a nobility, no less than is involved in such consecration.

That privilege, I said, brings with it its duties. *Noblesse Oblige!* When the Government trains your young friends at West Point, they know they are bound in honor for its flag to live and for its flag to die. Nor have many of them proved false to that requisition. When these colleges, which you represent, were established by pious men, or by far-seeing Governments, or by an aggressive Church.—when they gave to you the training and the companionship which make you what you are and will be,— you were bound in just the same responsibility. *Noblesse Oblige!* You could not, if you would, escape the obligation. And the Republic lives or dies according as we, and others like us, give to her or refuse to her this unpurchased service. There are enough who will go into her councils bribed by her gold. There are enough who will affiliate themselves in intrigues to sway her policy, in the hope of petty places for themselves or their friends.

Unless there are more who are driven into the service, which public spirit demands by the nobility of men, who would bear their brothers' burdens, the Republic dies. Enter upon life, and you will find with every day some new call made for your unselfish service. You are to improve the schools, or you are to mend the roads, or you are. to give strength to the church. Here must be a free library, and no one but you to see to it; there must be a hospital, and but for you the sick will die unattended, and the blind in darkness. Do not let us, who are your seniors, hear any such excuse from you as that " every man has his price ; " that " every hour must be coined ; " that " another man may do it as well as you." No man can do the work to which God calls you, but you yourself. And we, as we pass off the stage, expect and demand of you, who come after us, that you stand by the State and Church which have stood by you. Let us hear this resolution from the young men who follow us. Our privilege compels us, — *Noblesse Oblige !*

Men of my calling, trained to the one universal profession in the study of theology, — who may study all life, because our study is to draw men nearer to the God of life, — in the fascination of our own calling never fully understand why men engage themselves willingly in other walks of duty. To us all studies are open, and there is no science where we may not inquire. None the less do we see, however, that all men, of whatever calling, so far as they deal with these divine and infinite relations of man, — truth, beauty, justice, or life, — are all Knights of one Round Table, linked together in one great fraternity of duty, blessed by one privilege, and called by one call. That call is, to quicken and enlarge the life of the State, — the public spirit, in which the State endures. We stand by each other, shoulder to shoulder, in such endeavors ; or we encourage each other by distant signals, each from his lonely beacon. That these drudges in the crowded city may truly live; that these heathen in the polluted islands may truly live ; that this miser, heaping up rusty gold, may truly live; that these debauched profligates, wasted in lust, may truly live ; that the nation, not hampered by her useless acres, nor bound to earth by her mines of wealth, may truly live, — this is our office, an office which is our privilege. This is the

4

service in which we are united as servants of the liberal professions. It is the service to which we are called by Him who lived and died that men might have life more abundantly!

# IV.

## THE MIND'S MAXIMUM.

FEW men who have to do work with their brains, even in the humbler processes of such labor, grow to be forty years old without regretting that they were not taught, twenty years before, those arrangements and devices for husbanding their intellectual faculty, and making it as useful to them as possible, which they have been obliged to learn for themselves, without system, and often in the wreck of failure. There is nothing so much neglected in the universities, where they attempt to teach almost every thing, as the sciences of learning rapidly and of using readily what one knows. The rules and constitutions of Benedictines and of Jesuits show how much and how little care the lawgivers of such orders of students devoted to systematizing study. These directions are almost always superficial and empirical,

and, though by no means without value, nowhere rise to the dignity of a philosophical system of intellectual activity.  In our own time,
there has been a great deal said about "self-
culture," which has professed to give instructions
for intellectual culture.  But a treatise on self-
culture generally ends, as Dr. Channing's does,
in showing that it is very important to have the
mind well trained, and in good working order,
without telling how it is to be trained for keeping its working power at a maximum.  There
is also latent in most of such books the grave
error that a man cultivates his mind simply by
reading, — a process which, in fact, often involves a loss of mental efficiency.  This error
has gone so far, that in common talk a man is
praised for cultivating his mind, simply in proportion as he reads books of any graver character than novels.

Such errors are not made in either of the
other great lines of human activity.  In the
domain of bodily work, people understand that
the training of the body is one thing, and the
feeding it quite another.  When that periodical

cycle of interest in physical training comes round, through which just now we happen to be passing, nobody sends the young gymnast into a fruit-market, or to a *table d'hôte*, directing him to eat all he can, by way of educating his body. And the time has passed, in the other science of training the soul, when men thought it would attain its full power by rapt contemplation of God and heaven. It is only in the cultivation of the mind, that there is tolerated a general gorging: each teacher encouraged to force down as much as he can, and the pupil then turned loose, to bring his resources to bear as best he can, without a suggestion, even, as to methods of working power.

Yet the demand of the present time is especially for the utmost amount of intellectual work which can be extorted from educated men, and consequently for its utmost facility and method. There are not enough of them to do the world's work now; and the insufficient body of those who are detailed to this duty, ought to husband their mental resources to the utmost, and to bring them to bear with the most

recondite tactics. Let any professional man of
to-day amuse himself for an hour with his
grandfather's diary of his professional life. Let
him compare the letter a month received and
answered in the life of the last century, against
his own file of three or four hundred received,
indexed, and replied to within a like time. Let
him compare the grandfather's annual ride, by
his own horse-and-chaise power, to the " Convention of Ministers," when Election Week
came round, with his own annual attendance at
a year's directors' meetings, committee meetings,
board meetings, and trustees' meetings. Let
him look at the schedule of books attached to
his grandfather's will, called his "library," to
see that there are not so many in all as he has
been expected to give an opinion on in the
conversation of the last five years of life. Let
him count, in the diary, the number of public
opinions which his grandfather formed in ten
years of voting for Washington, Adams, Bow-
doin and Strong, against the opinions which he
has himself been compelled to form, and form
correctly, regarding foreign and home politics,

State administration, city, church, and school affairs; regarding water, gas, horse railroads, school-ventilation, foreign emigration, negro emancipation, and the rest, — opinions which he has had to enforce, and to carry if he could, at three or four special, city, State, and national elections every year. Any man who will make this contrast will see that this generation requires an amount of intellectual readiness, and a degree of economy in the right and righteous use of intellectual power, such as no generation has required before.

We have no hope of laying down the true system of the maximum of intellectual effort. But we do hope to show that teachers, of whatever grade, ought to give more attention than they have done to suggesting for their pupils systems so essential. To take a little instance : there is not an axiom in physics more absolutely settled than the fact that no mental labor of any sort should be attempted within the hour after a full meal. Yet it is only within a few years that the University at our Cambridge ceased to bid students recite within forty minutes after the beginning of breakfast, and within an hour after the beginning of dinner. What was as bad was, that half the college recited — or, shall we say, pretended to recite — before breakfast was served. The old monks, from whom the greater part of our college system has descended, at least knew better than this. In these details, matters are now better ordered at Cambridge. It is possible that the gymnasium and the trainer may introduce yet more improvements. We hear rumors sometimes of practical hints, given by professors there, of the way to bring mental faculty into play. And we are not without hopes that, as there has long been a course there on "The Means of Preserving Health," some teacher may introduce a course on "The Methods of Using Intellectual Power." Such a course comes fairly within the range either of theology, ethics, metaphysics, or hygiene; and whoever first does throw into system the results of thirty years of his own experience, and teach the arts, methods, and science of best husbanding and cultivating, and of most quickly and vividly

using, intellectual power, whether of the
meanest or finest quality, will earn the grati-
tude of the meanest and finest minds together,
and a claim to a share in whatever good they
may ever work for mankind.

I. In pointing out the relations of such instruction to the different lines of human science,
we must, with whatever regret, speak first of its
physiological relations. We beg the reader,
however, not, for this, to turn ruthlessly from
this paper, as if he had here only another divi-
dend from the assets of Sylvester-Grahamism,
or House-I-Live-in-ism. We are forced to speak
of physiology; but our chief object is to say
that that folly is now nearly exploded, which
mistook the severe treatment necessary (perhaps) for the cure of students in confirmed
dyspepsia, for the proper treatment of men in
health, eager to work, mentally, under the
requisitions of this time, up to the very top of
their steam. The dyspeptics may settle with
the doctors what is the proper treatment for
them. We neither know nor care. Our busi-

ness is with men in health, that they may keep their health, and that they may find out what is the highest amount of their working power, and may keep to that without overrunning it. We venture to say that, for them, any system of half-diet, of scales to weigh daily bread, of food marked by some invalid name, — any system, in short, which in any way suggests hospitals or convalescence, — is bad practice. On the other hand, we venture to say to the dyspeptics, that they had better leave the company of men working with their minds till they are well. It will not be long. There is always open, for instance, the army; and when on foot in the open air, we forget the doctor soon.

The dictum with regard to food, then, is probably that of one of our most judicious medical men, to whom this community is largely indebted, who used to say to his class: "In brief, gentlemen, you may eat what you choose, when you choose, and as often as you choose; only be careful not to look at your tongues after you have done." For as, in the highest stage which in this world we come to in the religious life, a man forgets he has a soul through ninety-nine out of a hundred of the hours which he crowds full of enterprise for the glory of God, so, in the lower plane of which we speak now, he forgets, by a corresponding law, that he has a body. The degree to which he remembers or forgets it gives an accurate measurement of its frailty or its health.

For all this, however, he has a body; and the ignorance of youth, which risks it sometimes to its ruin, is not the same grace as the confirmed habit of discipline to which we would lead youth, which uses it as not abusing it. They are, at the least, as different as is innocence from virtue. Man has a body. It is one of his tools. His mind is the other. Now, the Latin Grammar is very right in saying: "The mind itself knows not what the mind is;" which is as true of Spurzheim's mind as it was of Cicero's. But the mind does know, by this time, that, whatever it is or is not, it works by means of a physical arrangement called a brain, or a pair of brains. Let the question lie, then, what the mind is. Still, in discussing the discipline of its working power, we must say something, however unwillingly, on the physiological conditions of the brain, on the privileges to which it is entitled, and the cautions which it has a right to claim from those who would effect the most the most promptly, with an organ so exquisite and so delicate.

The familiar statement that the " brain is the stomach," or the " stomach is the brain," which we sometimes hear, would probably not satisfy the anatomists. But it expresses very conveniently some results of physiology and anatomy which all workmen ought to remember. The chief of them is this, that, at the moment when you have given the stomach its work to do, you have no right to call upon the brain, at the other end of the same system, to be working for you also. When you are journeying, you take assiduous care that your horse shall not be compelled to do any work in the hour after he has slowly eaten his grain. The horse has cost you money ; and, even in the poor business of his muscular action, you know that he needs all his vital resource for the single matter of getting

his grain in part stowed away. Because you
happen to be impatient, you do not risk his
health, which you have paid for. Now, it is
true that you never bought your brain at a
horse-market. It might not fetch a bid there.
Certainly it ought not, if you have no more
practical notion, after your experience of it,
than to set it hard at work while the whole
working power of your system has been pre-
engaged lower down. Consider what you have
done. You have poured together a pint of
coffee, three hot biscuits buttered, the lean
parts of two mutton-chops, and a slice of stale
bread, into the reservoir which contains your
provisions for the first six hours of the day.
You have done this by way of breaking the fast
of the night before. Give, now, to the officials
who have the present charge of those supplies
an hour's uninterrupted time after you have
done: do not embarrass them by constantly
sending down to ask what is seven times nine,
or what is the interest for four years and eleven
days on blank hundred and blankty-blank dollars at blank per cent. Give them that hour

of undisturbed work on their present business, and then start the engine slowly; and thank us, who have advised you, for the promptness and efficiency of its new revolution.

Without dabbling in the detail of physiology, we may say, simply, that one precise object for which you have eaten your breakfast is to give to this delicate organ, the brain, the compensation it needs for the work it did for you yesterday. You may call it wages, if you regard the brain as your servant; or food, if you regard it as your slave; or sympathy and encouragement, if you regard it as your friend. Whatever you call the breakfast, the fact is, that the brain lost in amount of substance yesterday just in proportion as you worked hard with it. The nice observations of a few years past have shown to a certainty that the brain loses elements, which may be detected as phosphates in the fluids of the body, just in proportion to the intensity of its exercise. The masterly argument with which you kept that drowsy jury awake yesterday cost you its weight in phosphate. The letter of entreaty which you wrote last night (which you

should have left till this morning) was well
put, succinct, and pathetic; and it cost you,
therefore, its weight in phosphate. Your calculation of the comet's orbit differs by two days
from Dr. Pape's. You have analyzed your
work, and, in a day's careful labor, have proved
to all men and angels that you are right and
that Dr. Pape is wrong. Yes, that is very fine;
but the tongs which you put into that white-
heat lost some little scales of iron as you turned
over and over the equations and formulas. The
triumphant calculation cost your brain just its
weight in phosphate. Do not cheat the servant
or the friend who has served you so. Or, do
you count him as a slave, do not cheat yourself by starving him. And if you mean to
work him in that same fashion to-day, let him
have new phosphates, exquisitely and carefully
elaborated from the coffee, the chop, and the
bread-and-butter; let the new and the old be
well introduced to each other, and on good
social terms, before you give the word for new
duty.

It is not simply new substance, however,

which the brain requires. While we know very little about its methods, we know that it has methods which it insists upon. We will not anticipate the physiologists so far as to say it is a Voltaic battery: but this is a guess so well sustained now that we might do that with reason ; and we may say that, in the particular matter with which we are dealing, it works with exactly the laws of a Voltaic battery. Those laws are now matters understood in daily practice. Bear them in mind. If you were De Sauty working the Atlantic Telegraph, seeking the highest power from your battery, and the most precise action, would you use the very same fluids to stimulate the plates month after month, regardless of the wear of the plates and the disintegration of the liquid? Not at all. You have not only to renew the plates at certain periods, but you have, at shorter periods, to renew the liquids. Of course you would never attempt to work without liquids in the battery. As well work without plates. Of course you would not be satisfied, even though you had the best double-combination improved

battery which science ever invented, to work
by splashing a little liquid, whatever might
come along, on the plates for a moment.
Though some result would undoubtedly follow,
it would not be the high-pressure, extreme-
tension result which you are in search of. You
would pour in, with the utmost care, the liquids
which had been prepared with the most accurate chemistry. And, even then, you would
have to wait for some moments, more or less,
before the battery would fully work on them,
or they on the battery, and the high action
begin. Now, whether the brain is or is not a
battery, let the physiologists settle. It works
precisely by these laws which we have stated.
In sleep, for instance, it is inactive, if the fluids
elaborated from food are not ruthlessly poured
upon it, in which case it acts in dream or night-
mare. Before breakfast, it is in no condition
for active work. When breakfast comes, still
it must wait till the elaboration of its precise
liquid is completed. When that is at length
poured on, grant the few moments, more or
less, of the electrician, and then you may draw

your sparks, lift your heavy weights, telegraph
to the other side of the world, or the other
end of time, at your pleasure.

With these mere hints, we close what we
have to say of the very foundation of our subject, however important that foundation may be.
In most of the popular frenzies on the connec-
tion of mind and body, some piece of successful
treatment of disease is seized upon, and held up
as the legitimate system to be pursued in health.
Because a shower-bath occasionally gives to
a disordered system the freshness and vivacity
which it had forgotten, people tell you to take
one every day, and that you shall be sure to be
fresh and alive. The experiment fails. Because a *bon vivant* gains spirits and energy when
he cuts off half his luxurious dinner, Sylvester
Graham tells him, virtually, that if he will give
up the other half he will have twice as much
spirit and energy. And, in physical exercise,
because a man works more lightly and happily
after a walk, or other exercise sufficient to pro-
mote digestion and renew appetite, we are told
to work like Hercules in a gymnasium, and to

walk like Captain Walker in the training-ground. All this is absurd. If a man wants to work with his mind, he only wastes food, time, and life by bringing his body up to the mark of a blacksmith's or a boxer's. He neither needs to run a mile in *five-thirty*, nor to lift six hundred pounds, nor to walk up to the house-top by the lightning-rod. He wants exercise enough to keep him in high spirits, good appetite, and that absolute health which almost forgets there is a body to be cared for. The truth is, that a prime condition of vivid intellectual labor is that one give as little attention as is practicable to the tools with which he works. And, just as the mower loses repute for mowing who is constantly setting his scythe anew, or stopping to sharpen it; and just as he advances more slowly than the more skilful workman who does not complain of his tools, — the mental artisan who works lightly in the harness with which it has pleased God to clothe his spirit, advances with most success and most rapidity. It is folly to pretend there are no tools. It is folly to leave them to rust in the meadow over night.

It is folly to pretend there is no harness. It is folly to leave the harness without oiling it. But it is worse folly to spend all one's life in sharpening one's scythe, or in beautifying the traces or the collar.

We shall leave, for a like reason, without any notice, the questions regarding diet: how the food should be concocted which is to renew the plates of our battery, if it be a battery; and how the liquids, which are to be poured on it to excite its motion. Bearing in mind the golden injunction which we have quoted, — that we may eat much as we please, if we do not make food too much the subject of after-meditation; that the brain-stomach is most likely to digest our food for us when we do not make the stomach-brain weigh it, analyze it, account for it, and justify it; resolving that we will not thus try to think cake and eat cake too, —we do not discuss the relative merits of coffee, tea, matté, cocoa, or guarana, in their province of reproducing brain, which is, according to Liebig, their duty in the economy of civilization. Swedenborg wrote his oracles on coffee; and so, they say, did Agassiz his. Most poor sermons are written on tea, and, they say, some good ones. We have read capital editorials which were written on shells; we have heard that the high law-officers in England are detected with ale when they are caught at luncheon; and we know that Anacreon says that the best is water. Into that discussion we do not go.

II. We have reached a much more interesting part of our subject, where, however, all the authorities in print begin to fail us sadly. We may call it the internal economy of mental action. It seeks light on the best methods and proportions of work, either in varying mental processes, or in holding steadily to one. It involves, also, the questions as to the real maxima of intellectual effectiveness. On these subjects the monkish authorities have but little to say. The truth is that their work did not admit of much variety. It was simply the steady plodding on of uncritical readers, or of self-satisfied writers, who were in no dread of criticism. The German scholars also have wide reputation as great workmen, but we are disposed to challenge that too. When it is said that Heyne worked twenty hours three days in the week, and twenty-four hours on the intermediate days, — and this is said of Heyne, — a quality of work is meant much of which does not deserve the name. These pundits go into their rooms, and call all that is done there work, if it only involve reading. The newspaper counts for work, or the last novel or review. We have known similar self-deception nearer home, but we have nothing to do with it in this paper. We are discussing simply the action of the mind which directly aims at some new evolution of truth, or some new presentation of truth evolved before. The student is at work if he is presenting truth in new forms to himself, or if he is attempting to present it in new forms to others. But, exactly as copying does not come within our idea of intellectual work, because the workman there only repeats for others truth already evolved, in an unchanged form, mere reading or acquisition of information undigested comes as little within it. For here the workman only repeats to himself the result of the study of others. The workman, in both cases, works mechanically. In fact, mere reading is the greatest of intellectual luxuries. If there is any difficulty in understanding an author, of course an element of labor comes in, as when one reads in a language not perfectly familiar to him. But where the reading is perfectly intelligible, it is not to be ranked as intellectual work. It will undoubtedly fatigue eye and brain ; but the fatigue to the brain is the very minimum involved in any mental action. As the German epicure said he could eat larks all day, any man or woman may say he can read all the time he can spare from his meals, his digestion, and his other physical exercises. If it tire his eyes, that is merely a bodily affair. We do not therefore take mere reading into the account of the mental effort which we are considering.

A popular writer[1] succinctly stated the moral aspect of the maximum of work in the following words, in a newspaper article : " No man has

---

[1] Mr. Thomas Drew.

a right to incur more fatigue in a day than the sleep of the next night will recover from."

As a general rule, we conceive that this statement is the true one. There are exceptions, or course, when generals must march their men by forced marches, but they are exceptions to be permitted with the greatest care. The intentional violation of the rule is simply suicide by inches. The man who wakes to-day conscious that he overworked yesterday, because he finds he is not up to yesterday morning's working mark, has run back just so far in his own life. There seems no moral distinction between the act, if it were intentional, and the act by which, instead of injuring his brains a little, he should injure them a great deal in blowing them away. The regular recurrence of night and day seems to be so adapted to the human constitution of mind and body, that we must put ourselves under regulations of this sort dependent upon it. And as no man eats one great breakfast Sunday, expecting to lunch Tuesday for the week, to take the week's exercise Wednesday, to dine once for all Thursday, to take a twenty-four hour siesta on Friday, and a protracted cup of tea Saturday, all to be followed by a week's night of sleep; as every man admits that the regimen of the body is to be regulated by cycles of twenty-four hours each, — we hold that every man must use his mind in the same way. It must come up to time, as the Ring says, every morning fresh and bright, as if, indeed, it were new-born, if we mean to get from it the maximum of vivacity and power. The great *tours de force* invariably prove this. A newspaper reporter will tell you of specific feats in which he wrote steadily, in the most fatiguing form of writing, perhaps for fourteen consecutive hours. So will turfmen tell you of horses who have been driven without stopping for as many. But neither of them will tell you that the week in which those hours were included came up to the average steady work of the mind, or the horse, concerned.

No more work is to be done in a day than the night's sleep will recover from. That is the first rule. So far the sun, Ammon Ré, is the lord of this business, as the Egyptians regarded him.

5

So much of subdivision is mapped out for
a man in the calendar as matter of morals.
And, as the calendar marks Sunday with red
letters for him, he is to throw that also out from
his list of working-days, except as the priests
in the temple profaned the Sabbath and were
blameless. If a man's profession make him work
on Sundays, — as does a daily editor's, or his
printer's, or a chorister's, or organist's, or other
minister's, — let him make allowance for that va-
riation by taking his rest-day on some other day
of the week: best on Saturday, so far as the
arrangements of modern life suggest the resting-
day for the exceptional classes we have named.
There is no difficulty in advancing thus far in
the regulation of working-time. But in further
subdivision, where we have the moral question,
the ground is more difficult, the lights less frequent, and the authorities are more at variance.

Dr. Andrew P. Peabody, an excellent guide,
tells us in his Discourse before the Divinity
School Alumni, that every man who works with
his mind "should have a vocation and an avocation." That is to say, to avoid the fatigue

of monotony, or the danger of any of the forms
of monomania, from despondency up to the
acme of that disease, let a man be sure that
his daily duty has, at' least, two sides to it.
When he has worked enough at the one, let
him work in turn at the other. Be it observed,
this is a rule for alternating forms of work.
We say nothing as yet of play. The rule, as
an empirical rule, proves itself true. It would
prove itself true in practice, even in the limited
view which our subject takes, — a much nar-
rower one than the broad view of professional
life which Dr. Peabody was considering. For
if we only regarded mental efficiency and vivacity, it would prove better for a man to have
two subjects of mental effort, which should engage him alternately, than one alone. As matter of practice, most thinkers, or most students,
would admit this. But what is the principle
on which this rule rests, — and how far may we
make the rule go? First, as to the principle.
Are there different sets of mental faculties, as
the phrenologists say, so bounded and contrasted
that it rests one set to have you put another set

in motion, — as they used to tell us that a blacksmith, after striking with his arms all day, rested himself with dancing? When, for instance, one has been loving his children intensely for an hour, does it rest him to do sums in the rule of three for an hour, and then will he rest himself more by remembering the roots of the Greek numerals for an hour more? We do not believe he will. We believe this whole theory of the rotation of mental crops to be a mistake. The true rotation is precisely akin to that of the rotation of vegetable crops. The old notion was, that the land which had been cultivated for wheat rested when you put it in clover, and rested more when you put it in turnips ; so that it was with perfect enthusiasm that in the fourth year it received wheat again, and that it then produced wheat as never before. The truth was, that that land never rested at all. The clover took up elements which the wheat had left, and the turnips found such as both had left. But if the clover and the turnips had been carried off the ground, when the wheat came again in the fourth year of the rotation to the dinner which had been warmed over twice for these different guests, it found but poor picking left. And it proves that the system of rotation, undoubtedly well founded, requires for its correct use that one or more years shall be virtually years of rest. The best rest is that which is given when a crop is planted, permitted to grow, and ploughed back into the ground. At all events, nothing must be carried, in the rest-year, from the field. We believe this to be just as true of intellectual croppings. You undoubtedly gain by varying your vocation with an avocation; perhaps you gain then by what we have heard called a " third," — some third pursuit, which may be called an avocation of the second power. But you have only a very limited line of relief in this direction. It is undoubtedly exhausted when you have come to the " third," — and very soon you must give to the soil you are drawing from the complete rest of a fallow, or of hours spent for its own re-creation only. It is probable that the impression that passive qualities are rested because others are at work, is false. The blacksmith does not rest himself by dancing, or reading, or playing checkers. He may *di-vert* himself thus, but he does not *re-create* himself. To re-create himself he is more apt to eat his dinner, to drink his tea, to smoke his pipe, or to go to sleep. In all which experiments but one, he shows his practical knowledge of physiology.

It is true that the facility with which different minds change from subject to subject, is one of the traits of character in which men are most unlike each other. We are the more restricted in our discussion of it. The word " versatility " has been invented to express a high degree of this facility. It is to be observed, however, that because Lord Brougham can discuss Natural Theology, Criminal Law, and any thing else in the Cyclopædia, with equal ease, *when he chooses*, it does not follow that he will choose to work on three such subjects in the same hour or in the same day. Our own conviction is that he will prefer to do all his work on one in one day, and all his work on another in another day, perhaps in another month or year.

All reputations for versatility are to be studied with reference to this distinction. The ease with which Mr. Charles Mathews or Mr. Proteus Love drops behind a table, and reappears instantly as an old woman instead of a young man, as we saw him just before, is indeed amusing to the spectator. But it is not a valuable accomplishment. Even as a bit of costume, the old woman's dress or the young man's would prove badly adapted for practical purposes. In the same manner, the versatility which works its wonders in mental work within an hour is a gift as amusing, and in some points perhaps proves convenient; yet the work it does is of but poor quality after the first change or two. Homer characterizes this quality, when he says of Margites, —

Πόλλ' ἠπίστατο ἔργα, κακῶς δ' ἠπίστατο πάντα.
"He knew a great many things, — but he knew all of them badly."

The versatility, however, of which Mr. James Martineau's various scholarly work seems so good an illustration, — of a mind which occupies itself heartily with one subject till it can make to the world some statement of real value regarding it, and then grapples with like force with a subject wholly different, is a versatility without which the world would lose almost the blessings which it wins from its heroes.

Work without interruption, then, while you work, till the day's task is done. That is the rule for gaining the maximum of the best work of which the particular mind concerned is capable. Between the vocation and the avocation there is fair opportunity for a pause, which may be hours long if necessary. But when work is once begun on one subject, it should not be suspended till the day's contribution has been rendered. In "Miss Martineau's Travels" is Dr. Channing's statement on this point, — not repeated, if we remember, in his Life. He says that the first hour of composition is to him very painful, — that the work grows easier and easier as the hour advances, but that only at the beginning of the second hour does he begin to work at ease and cheerfully. The experience again reminds us of what we see in a Voltaic battery, of the irregular, almost spasmodic labor of the cells when work begins, and the gradual regularity, and even passion, which in a short time the process obtains. Now the practical remark of importance is that, if the work be thoroughly interrupted, all this initial difficulty has to be passed through again. It is exactly as if the battery be lifted from the liquid long enough for its plates to dry. The bore who says, "I will not interrupt you, I only want two minutes," speaks like a fool. The two minutes involve as completely a new initiation of the mental process as two months would do. He might as well say, "I am not going to break your mirror into pieces far apart, — I will only separate the bits by a crack of a millionth of an inch." You do not want the mirror broken at all. And you must not have the mental process broken at all, whether of mathematics, of logic, of historical research, of the reconstruction of lost historical truth, of illustration by poetry, or of composition for conviction, if it is to be your best process. It must begin and work steadily to its own self-appointed close. There is not the slightest uncertainty when that close comes. You know it yourself when you feel it. And then, after such pause as you like, the *a*-vocation must begin.

It is said that the musical critics can tell in Mozart's Requiem at what points he went to sleep in its composition, and was waked by his wife to begin again. We have no doubt this is true. A truly sympathetic criticism would show of almost any fine literary composition where the work was suspended and where it began again, — where Homer nodded. If in any case this seems impossible, it is probably because the work is all mosaic: the mental process was broken so often, that it is patched all through, and nowhere rises to the severity or the simplicity of an intaglio in an unbroken gem.

This principle of intellectual effort seems to us to decide the question as to the number of a-vocations, or sides to a man's daily duty. Two sides will probably exhaust his working-power for a day. The "third" to which we have alluded should, in our opinion, be thrown wholly into the part of the day allotted to

amusement, and should be of no character re-
quiring energy, will, or vivacity even. It ought
not even to involve physical fatigue beyond the
requirements for the day's bodily exercise. Do
not play chess for a diversion to intellectual
labor. Do not read history merely because you
like to. Do not read any thing grave enough
to require what Capel Lofft calls re-flection, —
the turning back over the passage to determine
whether you agree with the author or no. Do
not persuade yourself that a fatiguing walk will
rest your brain. It is only so much drain on
phosphates of the muscles, and you must repro-
duce phosphate for the brain before you can go
to work again. Do not pretend to be virtuous,
in short, by passing any labor into currency as
if it were play. You had better go to the
theatre, or to the opera, if these are not as hard
work to you as they seem to be to most per-
formers. Play cards. Dance. Listen to music.
Laugh. Sit on a rail-fence and see how green
the grass is, and how blue the sky. New England undertook, a generation ago, to smuggle
the Lyceum into the place of the drama, and

grind a few axes in the way of instruction when she pretended to be amusing her work-people. Human nature took its revenge, however. And it has been years since a Lyceum Lecture of the popular class instructed anybody, called for any thought, or indeed fatigued any one but the lecturer. All which is as it should be.

We have said that the time to stop work showed itself. As soon as the vital current enlivening study or composition flags, this time has come. If the student looks at his watch, or shakes his hour-glass, or in any way feels mistrust of his subject or himself, the battery is losing power, and the direction of its activity should be changed. This is the time for the a-vocation to come in. We need not say that the more unlike its processes to those of the vocation, the better for all concerned. If one have involved writing, let the other be mainly reading. If the one have been fine art, let the other be mathematical, or historical, or, in a word, as different as it can be. In our judgment, by the time the a-vocation rings its alarm-bells in its turn, and asks, as the Jacquard loom does in like junctures, for a change of color, it is time for the workman to stop mental work for that day. Let his exercise begin, or his diversion, his social life, or that general *potpourri* of undetermined existence in which most of us spend most of our hours ; directed not by ourselves but by destiny, — by the post-office, the almanac, the pig escaped, the cows in the cornfield, the agreeable Englishman who has come with a letter of introduction, or the unfortunate missionary to the Ojibways who wants to know how he is to educate three promising young men. The day's mental work is done, when the first mental a-vocation after the vocation begins to drag.

It is perfectly idle to attempt to say how long the day's mental work will continue before this limit is attained. It will vary with different minds, of course, and it will vary in the same mind, with the class of work done, and the degree of concentration required. The *tours de force* of which the human mind is capable are so extravagant that they can hardly be overstated. A hard-working physician in an epi-

demic will keep on his beat twelve hours,
working down two or three horses in that time
in his duties in a large city.  But he is committing
suicide all the time, and in this case scarcely by
inches.  The gentlemen of the bar sit in their
offices, or in court, nearly as long, for continued
periods.  But much of each day is not work in
that duty.  Our own observation of as broad
range of lives as have left us their memoranda,
would decide that three hours is as high a maximum as an average mind can seek, for the
average of its concentrated daily effort, of six
days' work in a week, and fifty-two weeks in a
year.  This is Sir Edward Lytton's statement;
Scott's was even lower than this.  The British
Commission on Education has often reported,
what we have no doubt is true, that with children, at the end of three hours' faithful study,
the power of acquiring is, in general, at the end
for that day.  That is to say, the child could
learn in three hours, well used, all that it does
learn in the six you keep it in school.  We have
no doubt this is true for children.  We should
put the acquiring power of men and women

rather higher, perhaps; but the average of all kinds of highly concentrated mental work is probably fully stated as three hours a day.

But alas! in saying that the man who works with his brains ought, for the best work which he can do, to work on only two lines of work every day, we do but demand an impossibility, if we be speaking of modern civilization. Perhaps they work so in Arcadia, though Dr. Wordsworth makes no mention of any clergymen, lawyers, or critics whom he found there. We have heard it said that in Charleston, South Carolina, before that city and State were included in the organism of the world, no man did but one thing in a day. At dinner you conversed on the day's employment. "I," said one, "went to Russell's for my umbrella, which I left there yesterday." "I," said another, "called at the news-room." "I," said a third, "made my compliments to Mr. Frazer, and saw his last picture." And the man who had done one thing in a forenoon deserved well of his country and posterity. Now that South Carolina also manures her fields, pays her laborers, shoots her voters, and approaches modern civilization in other points of practice, good and bad, there is left no such simplicity of civilization anywhere. The man who has brains, who should start on the determination that he would every day devote himself to two subjects only, would soon be shut up by his neighbors in the same palace with those who have none. Men must ' devote thought, and a great deal of thought, to a very wide circle of inquiries and occupations as a single day's work goes by. One cannot be Saint Bernard, or Duns Scotus, if he would, in a world which has advanced into the nineteenth century of the enlivenment of its life. To speak only of the invention of the post-office, — of which the advantages have never been so demonstrated as to leave it beyond question whether the curse it inflicts is not greater, — correspondence alone is enough to destroy the ideal system of daily mental activity which we have tried to describe.

" Correspondence is the burden of modern civilization," says Saint-Marc Girardin. He is describing the life of luxury which the first families of Rome led in their sea-shore homes in the centuries which Gibbon calls the happiest in the history of the world. On the other hand, most men of affairs tell us to-day that it is personal presence only which moves men now, letters going so easily where printed circulars go of course, into the waste-basket, or more directly into the fire. Yet the world has not yet learned this truth; if it be truth, and correspondence is still one of our greatest burdens. It is a burden which precisely illustrates the danger which we have described, of cutting off one mental process to begin again on another; of leaving to dry the supposed plates of the mental battery, before we set them to work again. It is far more fatiguing to the mind to write ten letters on different subjects of importance, than to write one on the same subject of the same length as all the ten. The change involved of method, of style, of familiarity, of recollections, calls so severely on the mental power employed as to drain it to the utmost. It would therefore be better, unquestionably,

always to answer a letter as soon as it is received, while the mind is still occupied with the
subject, thus avoiding break and jar. Letter
and answer would then cost only the fatigue
of hand required in writing. But this would
shock people's prejudices in favor of second
thoughts, there being in the world a suspicion
that rowen is sometimes worth more than June
hay. And it would make correspondence fatally brisk. The railroads are bad enough, but
how terrible life, if every letter brought its
echo by return mail! The practical way for us
to regain the paradise of our ancestors in these
matters would seem to be to answer our letters
in the moment which received them, and then
lay the answers by for a month before we
posted them. One hard-pressed friend suggests
to us that the invention of small note-paper is
the providential remedy. We have never seen
any small enough to cure the disease. Another
studies the Duke of Wellington's despatches,
in hope of attaining brevity. Another has
blanks by which a secretary furnishes uniform
answers to all the people who would like his

recommendation for Chief-Justice, or, if they cannot be that, would be glad of a subordinate commission in the quartermaster's department. But the system of blanks goes only a very little way in relief. Another used a manifold letter-writer for his letters of affection, and sent them in triplicate to different friends. But this plan was upset when he had one returned by a wounded spirit not appreciated. Members of Congress sometimes detail their wives to write their autographs for them. Mr. Fillmore used the best plan we know, if the thing is to be done at all, in dictating to a phonographic reporter his letters. They were then written out at the reporter's leisure, signed, and posted; yet the original copies of the letters were preserved in the phonographic notes. Sixty letters of average length could perhaps thus be dictated in an hour; but we should say that an hour of such work would be all the concentrated work any man ought to do in a day. The most effective man we ever knew never answered any letters at all. All that he wrote were the letters which affairs made necessary for the communication of information to his fellow-laborers. For the rest, let them come and see him, — as, alas! they did. It will probably be in this way eventually that the " burden of modern civilization " will be tipped off its back into the sea.

We need not apologize for this excursus on letter-writing, for the illustration it furnishes of the difficult conditions imposed on mental effort by modern barbarism is an illustration which covers very wide ground. Correspondence is the most oppressive of a series of demands made on men of affairs which interrupt the regularity of mental effort for which any system provides. And no study of the subject is in the least adequate, which does not allude to such external demands and interruptions. They must be provided for as well as the mind's personal and immediate requisitions. If they cannot be resisted or avoided, the reply made to the requisitions of the mind itself must be adapted, as far as possible, to their rapacity. We are not bound to travel into detail to discuss the adaptations which will be found the most successful. Every department of mental effort has to furnish its own; the tricks by which different hunted hares escape from the hounds let loose upon them in the barbarism in which we live, — the methods by which men doing their own duty meet, in contest or in submission, the invaders who ask them also to do theirs. Nor is it fair to speak as if all such invasions of a man's own plan of life ought to be avoided or evaded. In a world where our whole duty is to bear each other's burdens, it ill becomes any man of us to choose the particular way in which he will bear them, — the particular yoke which he will carry.

It is evident that, if one is to shift from point to point among a multitude of important cares in such complex affairs, the maximum of working time must be reduced, even below the poor three hours which we have given as the average of daily exertion. Baron Rothschild, who may be supposed to have arranged as nicely as any man can the methods for disposing rapidly of demands made on his thought, is said to meet them thus. He stands in a central office, in his place of affairs, where he can speak, if necessary, to his heads of department.  Those who have personal business with him are bidden to prepare in writing what they would say; they are introduced, and give to him or read to him the memorandum.  He answers; and the conversation, if any is necessary, follows, both standing. Brevity is attempted by the two expedients of a standing position and of written inquiry.  How necessary this is, any clergyman will say who has known a visitor take three hours in saying he wants to be married.  On the other hand, the value of personal presence is not lost, and the assistants, if necessary, are within call. Thus a hundred visitors, perhaps, are disposed of in a forenoon.  Concentration could hardly go farther.  We have described these details to say that it would evidently be impossible to work in that way, even up to our poor little average of three hours daily.  The more varied the subjects of work so highly concentrated, the shorter must its period necessarily be.

Of the palliatives possible for the relief of the pressure of such work as falls on the student or other literary workman, we do not speak in detail, because every condition of mental activity must of necessity provide its own. The transferring of the mechanical operation of writing, by those who have much work of composition, to the hand of an amanuensis, is the only one of these expedients which we are to speak of here. It does not seem well to use this relief to the full, as did an alderman of one of our chief cities, who, confident that he could always hire a reader to read for him, and a clerk to write for him, neglected to acquire for himself the two accomplishments of writing and reading. There are purposes of both accomplishments which cannot be attained by proxies. So this officer found, when, in an attempt to escape from the arrest which threatened him, because his various writings were so inconsistent with each other, he arrived at the fork of two roads, looked sadly at the finger-post, whose guidance was useless to him because he was without his reader; and so returned to meet the sheriff, and to acknowledge that there were occasions when one must do his own reading, as he had found before, by the state of his bankbooks, that he had better have done some of his own writing. Sentimental or exacting correspondents, too, are apt to expect that a letter shall be in the handwriting of the author. To meet this difficulty, the English offices have clerks in readiness, who, in three days after a change of ministry, are able to write in the handwriting of the new officials, and to execute for them their "private and confidential memoranda." Without going into such niceties, it may be said that any duty so mechanical as the mere forming of letters into words is probably better done by a young person whose whole attention is turned to it, than it can be by the person who is also engaged in determining what the words shall be. We have no doubt, therefore, that, on the whole, the employment of an amanuensis improves the quality of the work performed. It is very true that, when the experiment of dictating is first tried, the luxury of the ease it gives is apt to be so great that it tends to looseness and verbosity of style; for there is no better check on sesquipedalianism than the necessity of writing down one's sesquipedalian words for one's self. And, in the beginning, if one is lying on a sofa, and using another's hand, he puts in his long words and long phrases and unnecessary sentences, in the mere luxury of freedom, as the schoolboy cavorts and plunges as he first rushes out into the open air. But this is but the incident of a beginning; and, with a little discipline and criticism, any man can learn to write with the pen of an amanuensis in the same style as with his own. Some of Scott's best novels were written by the hand of others; some by his own. We would challenge the most exquisite criticism to discern between the two classes from the mere internal evidence afforded by their composition.

We can perfectly well hear the whine or the snort of indignation with which conscious genius has put by our suggestions in this paper, long before reading to this point, where we close. Conscious genius is very apt to say that it must work without rules. It has a good deal to tell about the tides of inspiration; and it is prone to

6

suppose that those tides are very irregular. It will ridicule the possibility of any science of mental effort; it will say that man must wait till he is inspired; and that until he is inspired all effort is vain. It says a great deal more on this subject, but in this dictum is the pith of the whole. Now, we are willing to own that we know nothing of the methods of genius except as we read of them in the lives of men of genius. But from those authorities we have to remark that if Goethe and Schiller, Walter Scott, even Byron and Bulwer, are men of genius, — not to go outside our own generation, — genius is as glad to work under absolute, fixed, and methodical conditions as is any hod-carrier. Even Byron, we say; for when Byron was engaged upon a poem, he knew perfectly well that it would not finish itself, but that his persistent will must finish it. The extraordinary amount of work he did finish in his short career is a monument to the persistency and steadiness of his working power. And we doubt if there be any touchstone more certain to distinguish between real genius and

Brummagem, than is the test which determines whether the mind in question is fresh, vivid, and in true condition for effort on every blessed morning given it by God ; or whether it can only boast certain fungous growths of gaudy color, but of most perishable substance, — which spring up on some mornings, and are nowhere to be found on others, — lawless and irregular, and therefore, if not quite worthless, quite untrustworthy.

The truth is that all mental effort, like all bodily effort, must fulfil the conditions of effort which God has imposed. This is as true of the highest efforts of divine poetry, as it is of the daily-bread work of the mere artisan of letters, who makes no pretence to genius or inspiration. We have been speaking, thus far, only of the two tools which are employed — the body and the mind — in such endeavor. But for the soul which employs them, if they are to be kept at their full power, there must be constant accessions of the Life from which the soul is born. It is Life which bends the fingers to the pen ; it is Life which drives the pen along the page ; it

is Life which makes the page live and teach its
lesson.   This Life of the soul must be renewed
and increased with every day of the soul's effort, or the page at length ceases to glow, just
as the fingers fail to grasp the pen.   The soul
must be, indeed, new-born to its daily work as
each day comes round.   The soul must each
day reassert its mastery over body and mind,
without which they are only two rebel slaves
setting in uproar the whole of the soul's kingdom.   We have said enough, perhaps, to show
that, for full mental power, this empire of the
soul must be a stern one.   The soul must deny
the body in its appetites of meat, of drink, even
of sleep, and of play.   It must cut off the stim-
ulants which the body would like.   It must insist on the repose without which the body dies.
We have seen also the restraints and the commands which it imposes on the mind.   The mind
would gladly run in a thousand directions in
the morning's effort ; and the soul grimly holds
it to one duty, or, at the most, to two.   We
see, again, that the soul does not let off either
servant to a holiday because they choose to beg

for it. When the hour of work comes, they
work; when it is at end, they stop. Whether
they like to work, or like to stop, the soul
makes the decision. For such absolute empire,
the soul needs new tides of Life daily. And
God has been pleased to grant such tides, re-
curring with the regularity of his own sunlight
if the soul accedes to the conditions. If the
soul uses to his glory the Life of to-day, under
the conditions which he has fixed for its various
exertions, he gives new Life for the duties of
to-morrow. The faithful, patient soul working
with him for his infinite designs finds itself new-
born as each morning struggles up the sky,
and, with the freshness of new birth, enters on
the new day's duties, — "as a little child"
indeed. But unless the soul accept the conditions, and unless it work in the Father's work,
it has no such renewal, and it has no continued
victory; any Hercules with whom it wrestles
can lift it from the ground, and, with all its
struggling, it can get no new strength for
conflict. Vital power for the objects of life;
vital power sufficient to hold in constant check

the vagaries of the mind and the appetites of
the body; vital power, again, sufficient to reani-
mate every morning a mind which has new
duties to undertake, and a body which is to
fulfil meekly an imperial will, — is gained only
at the fountain of Life. He has most of that
power who drinks deepest at the fountain. He
who never drinks — the Machiavel or the Napoleon — finds, before he is done, that body
and mind cannot be driven up to the behests of
the will. He who works with God has God's
breath to renew him every day. He who works
without God finds his body give way just when
he needs it, or his mind disobedient when a
crisis comes. For his vital power is diminished
by his every victory; while the faithful child
of God receives the promise, and with every
day has " Life more abundantly."

## V.

## A THEOLOGICAL SEMINARY.

SOME school of theology is allied to almost every one of our larger colleges, in more or less close relations. Most of the colleges, indeed, were established by one or another ecclesiastical body. In the lists published in the almanacs and elsewhere, they will be found marked with the letters B., R. C., E., P., and the rest, to indicate that they are under Baptist, Roman Catholic, Episcopal, Presbyterian, or other control. In many of the older colleges, the original plan was the training of young men for the Christian ministry. In the more recent instances of colleges thus fostered, the wish is rather to protect boys from the proselyting of other sects; to give them a direction towards the ministry, and such an inclination for it as may be followed up in the theological seminary or college distinctively so-called. The academical college is no longer made a place for the formal study of theology. Every denomination of Christians has its own institutions for that special purpose. Special societies for education are formed, to supply them with students. The Presbyterian Church in each of its organizations, North, South, and " United," maintains such societies for assisting in the education of young men in these schools. The largest of these, that of the Presbyterian Church North, expends nearly a quarter million annually in this service. The American Education Society, in similar service, expended twenty-eight thousand dollars last year ; and the similar society of the Reformed Dutch Church, thirteen thousand dollars. The various beneficiary funds which the Unitarians apply to like service, afford about ten thousand dollars a year for this purpose. Under such auspices, there are now in this country just one hundred theological schools, existing either as independent institutions or as the theological departments of universities.

What is the reason why young men do not go to these institutions in much larger numbers ?

The reason, I suppose, is two-fold. First, an objection lies against the method supposed to be pursued in the theological school. Second, an objection lies against the profession to be pursued as the result of this method.

I am certain that both these objections rest on insufficient grounds; and I propose to discuss them both, giving most space to the first. The objection is taken on a limited view of theological schools as they were: it is certainly not to be sustained by any adequate view of the better theological schools of America, or the schools of Germany, as they are.

If we could look in on the free conversation of some literary club or friendly gathering of seniors in any of our colleges, and hear the familiar talk on this subject, we should hear it said, first, that the young man who goes to a theological seminary goes pledged in advance to certain convictions, of which he has never examined the grounds satisfactorily. To make his training at the seminary of any practical use to him, he has got to say, at the end of the course, that he believes in each and all of certain

6*

formulas of doctrine, regarding which he is, at this present moment, only partially informed. It would be said that no such implied pledge restricted him in going to a law school or a medical school. He might believe opium to be a good drug in practice, or a bad drug; and yet no professor or school would follow him into the world to stigmatize his practice. He might come out from a law school wholly ignorant of nine-tenths of the studies pursued there; still, when he nailed up his shingle, no president of the law school would send messages after him, to say that his doctrine of mortmain was faulty, and that he was quite unsound in the theory of the civil law. The young doctor or the young attorney, it would be said, is left to stand or fall on his own merits.

But a young clergyman, these seniors would tell us, has a very different career in the professional school. Whether it be a school of thirty-nine articles, of twenty, or of five, he is expected from the beginning to come out, squarely and loyally, the supporter of them all. So far as he has received money from any education society to carry him through the expenses of his course there, he is under a pledge of honor, if not of verbal contract, to do the duty for which they pay this money to prepare him. And, if he is under no such formal pledge, his difficulty is the same. If, as he goes forward in his studies, he should doubt even the least tittle of the formulas put down in the books, — if he should think modern science had something to say which in these books is neglected, — the officers of the school would mark his dissent. It would be their duty, indeed, to do so. And, go where he might, they would — as from their point of view they ought to do — follow him up with letter or warning to this, that, or another synod, consistory, consociation, or association, to say that, though of admirable moral character, he was unsound in faith.

Now, young men do not like to enter on a course of study which, as they suppose, is thus hampered.

The next thing we should hear said, in such talk of seniors, would be, that there was nothing to study in " theology " that any man was much

interested in.   We should hear that a man must
"get up" a new language, — namely, Hebrew,
— while he knew he was not really master of
Greek, Latin, or the modern languages.   Then
we should be told that the rest of the time at
a theological school is spent in studying Greek
and criticising the New Testament; in writing
sermons and in hammering over Calvin's In-
stitutes.   This is about the popular idea which
most seniors have of studying theology.   The
men who have really heard the gospel-trumpet
sound, who know in their own hearts what the
Holy Spirit is because the Holy Spirit has spoken
to them, may have courage to take on the armor
thus offered to them, because they are told it is
useful armor.   Many of them do take it on; but
the majority of men solicited to take it, refuse.
They are Christian men, born again into the
divine life, as truly as are the young men who
go into the schools of theology.   But they hesi-
tate before attempting more Latin and Greek,
before launching upon Hebrew, before spend-
ing three years on what seem to them merely
technical studies.   They say what is true, that

there are many ways in which a man can work for the kingdom of God outside the pulpit; and that, if the pulpit require this preparation, other men may take it, but they will not. They enter upon some other profession.

Now, in answer to the impression which is popular among seniors, and which we have attempted thus to describe in its detail, I write this essay, to show in brief what a theological school is, and what it is not, when it is at work on a true footing. I say, in the outset, that such a theory of a theological seminary as I have described is a gross caricature on any theological seminary in this land. And I say, next, that when a first-class theological seminary of one of the liberal communions is contrasted with such a theory, every one of the objections which young men make to such institutions without knowing what they are, disappears.

First, as to the subjects studied. I venture the statement that all the great questions of modern discussion in which the young life of this country is specially interested, are nowhere studied in America so thoroughly as in its best theological seminaries.

Ask at the bookstores what those questions
are, or ask the secretary of a debating club.
The answer will be, first, that all the questions
regarding the creation of the world and the origin of man are the leading questions, —evolution, protoplasm, Darwinism as, for convenience,
people say.  Every wide-awake senior has read
Darwin, or the reviews of Darwin, — Mivart,
perhaps : he has read a few articles on the theo-
ries discussed by these gentlemen ; and the subject involved has been the subject of the familiar
discussion of the philosophical circles among
young men.

Now, where is a man to study this subject?
Where, in the first place, can he get the books
about it, — German, French, and English?  He
will find them in a well-furnished theological
library.  He will not find them anywhere else.

In the second place, if he wants to find any
professor vitally interested in the study, who
will manfully introduce it into his courses, and
give the last word of science with regard to it,
as well as the view which science has taken of it
for twenty-five hundred years, he must seek

that professor in a theological seminary. He may find the man in what is called a scientific college; but he will not find there any course of lectures devoted to such subjects. The bread-and-butter studies pursued there do not permit much use of time in speculation. Precisely the line of speculation in which at this moment the world is most interested is, from the nature of the case, — because it is speculation, and is not what is called practical, — shut out from all the American schools except the theological seminaries. They are, and for a long time must be, our only schools of pure philosophy.

Take another set of questions, the questions of race, on which all young men of intelligence of our times think a great deal and talk a great deal. Chinese question, African question, Catholic question, — they all hinge on questions of race. Who studies these questions of race? Do the lawyers study them? Not they; they are no affair of theirs. Do the medical schools? Scarcely; the pulse of a Calmuck and the pulse of a Hottentot beat in much the same way. The theologians do study them; they have to study them. Dr. Clarke's book on "The Ten Great Religions" is based on his lectures as a professor of theology. Dr. Everett's studies of Confucius are studies made for his classes in theology. "The Ethnic Religions," as they are called, which involve the full study of the relations of the races to each other, are studied in the theological seminaries, and nowhere besides.

Then there are the social-science questions, as people call them, for want of a better name. These occupy largely the attention of young men: questions of the relations of classes to each other, of labor to capital, of poverty to wealth, of emigrants to native citizens, of prisons, of punishment, of the "social evil," of the relief of pauperism, and other questions of this class. All men of sense are interested in these questions, — nay, all men of sense have to deal with them in life. Now, with regard to these questions, as with regard to the questions of the theory of creation, the books of reference alone are not to be found outside a well-furnished public library, collected with a view to the study. No law library contains such books, though in a broad sense it ought to. Social science is a specialty which thus far in this country has not made large collections. The young man interested in the discussions it involves will have to go to a well-furnished theological or university library to get his materials. And a theological seminary of the first class is the only place where he will find many persons interested in the same inquiries. He will find them there. He will find one or more professors personally well-informed in the details of the subject. He will find fellow-students who make it their special study; who propose to themselves the struggle with the blunders and evils of society as their work in life. Much of the student life and vital interest of a theological school is given to the methods and direction of such a struggle.

Now, I do not pretend that a young man entering on a course of theology at most theological seminaries would be permitted to choose simply such philosophical or practical studies as these, — which happen to attract young men, — and to pass by other studies in the curriculum.

What I wish to show is, that, in the curriculum of a well-furnished seminary, the very topics of philosophy most interesting to the public mind now occupy a very large place, though they be shielded and concealed from the public eye under such old-fashioned and academic phrases as "systematic theology," and "philosophy of religion." I will attempt now to unravel some of the other phrases, which, in the programmes of the schools, cover over a set of interests which all young men of intelligence share.

"Ecclesiastical history" is a great bugbear. "They have to spend so much time in ecclesiastical history." Popularly, in the average student mind, it is supposed that this is the study of lists of popes, of the dates in which Scotch synods sat, and of the order of the apostolic succession of Bishop Colenso and of the Rev. Mr. Knickerbacker. The truth is that ecclesiastical history is the history of the world, studied on the side of ideas rather than on the side of forms or statistics. History studied as Gibbon or Milman or Buckle or Lecky or Carlyle or Michelet study it, is ecclesiastical history. History studied in its outside or pictorial form, as Livy studies it, or Suetonius, or Richard of Devizes, or Hume or Prescott, is only an auxiliary to ecclesiastical history. Now, we need only refer to the real and lasting popularity of such books as Stanley's "Lectures on Church History," to show that the philosophical or ideal method, the only true and comprehensive method, is at the same time the method which really interests intelligent people. And here again, as before, I have a right to say that philosophical history is scarcely studied anywhere else in this country but in the better arranged theological seminary. The School of History, in Cornell, and the classes at Charlottesville, Va., are the only striking exceptions which I remember. So far from its being a study encumbered with detail of the methods of administration of the so-called "Church" of its time, it is very indifferent to such chaff, which gets itself forgotten very speedily. Dealing with such subjects as the Puritan Revolution in England, the Reformation in all its forms, the civilization of the north of Europe, the abolition of

slavery in the Roman Empire, the establishment
of the civil law, the diffusion of letters over the
world, — to name only three or four essential
points of consideration, — it is wholly impossible
that " ecclesiastical history " should be either a
dry or an unpractical study.

" Homiletics " again.    " Who, in his senses,"
says the average senior, "would study homiletics ? "    Well, I confess I am tempted to ask
what dean of a theological school in his senses
would put an old-fashioned word like " homiletics " into his programme of study ; or rather
a word like this, which was never in fashion.
Homiletics is the science of address : the science, so far as it can be put in science, by which
such men as Beecher and Wendell Phillips and
Charles Finney and Newman Hall and Frederic
Robertson and Charles Spurgeon affect in speech
their fellow-men, when they want to affect them.
Is it, or is it not, worth while to learn any thing
about that ?    Is that, or is it not, an interesting
study ?    To the average American student,
whose duty and destiny it is to move throngs of
men by the way in which he shall state to them

the truth, is it, or is it not, an important study?
But people say, " Homiletics sound like ' homily,'
and homilies are supposed to be dull!" No
matter what it sounds like: it is the science of
address. I never understood that anybody who
sat under the preaching of Ward Beecher or
Robert Collyer, the chiefs of homiletics just
now, found their preaching dull. Precisely because they knew something of homiletics, was
their preaching vital and entertaining.

I have before me the programme of the work
of the Theological Seminary at Cambridge,
where the "homiletics" are under the charge of
Prof. Everett, a gentleman who is one of the
few poets who are at the same time writing
metaphysicians. He is the man who has written
the one thorough statement of "The Science of
Thought" which has appeared in the English
language, so careful and accurate is his process
of reasoning. On the other hand, he is a born
poet, and sees the natural illustration of every
spiritual truth on the instant that the truth
asserts itself. That man, by good fortune, is
placed in the position of teaching young men

how to address audiences. Does any one who ever heard him, suppose that his presentation of that subject will be antiquated or dull?

And yet again I am tempted to ask, What place is there, after a man has left college, where he will be taught any thing of this essential business of addressing other men, except in a theological seminary? Certainly not in a law school, unless by good luck there is a spirited debating club among the students. Certainly not in a medical school. The doctors suffer till the day they die, from their inability to tell other men in public speech what they want to say to them. The chairs of the better theological seminaries alone supply this necessity; and they veil it under the unintelligible and disregarded title of the "homiletics."

There remain, of the studies of a well-appointed theological school, the criticism of the Bible and the science of ethics. These are unquestionably those at which the average senior, whom we have tried to describe, looks most suspiciously. Like a horse free in the pasture, he sniffs at the salt in the proffered measure, but determines, on the whole, that he prefers freedom without salt, to salt with a halter. He throws up his heels in the luxury of life without a tether, and gallops to the farther part of the enclosure; and his freedom ends in such liberty as he may find in a lawyer's office, or within sound of a doctor's bell, or as a principal of an academy!

What, then, is the critical study of the Old Testament and the New? It is the scientific, philosophical, manly study of a series of books which, as any Christian man believes, nay, knows, are of the very first importance to the world. And does any Christian man really say that he means to get along with any thing less than the scientific, philosophical, manly study of these books? Does he really mean to take his opinion of them at second hand, — and at second hand, perhaps, from very questionable or very ill-educated teachers? If a man really means that he knows more and better than is taught in the Sermon on the Mount, or that he can come nearer God than the Saviour brings him in the fourteenth chapter of John, that is one thing. That man may, with a certain con-

sistency, excuse himself from careful and adequate study of the Bible; but even in that con-
sistency there is a lamentable confession: "I
know very little of the Bible; therefore I do
not want to know any more." But, not to
inquire into the duty or the choice of that
man, — for other men, for men who have found
Jesus Christ to be their living help, and the
Holy Spirit the true leader of life, — is it a
natural or a consistent thing for them to say
that they are satisfied with a Sunday-school
knowledge of our indifferent version of the
Bible, and that they will not attempt to extend
that knowledge by a systematic or critical study
of it in the original? To say the very least,
have such men a right to pronounce, à *priori*,
that such study must be functional, formal,
and dull?

To speak very briefly of the last fifty years
alone. The opening of the Egyptian hierogly-
phics has made a new thing of the five books ascribed to Moses; the opening up of the Assyrian
and other Eastern inscriptions, and the daily reports of researches and travels in the East, have

made a new thing of the study of the historical books of the Old Testament. The emancipation of Christianity from the dogmas of the darkest ages has reopened the whole subject of the person, nature, and character of Christ. Seeley's "Ecce Homo," Renan's "Jesus," Furness's book with the same title, Parker's "Ecce Deus," Derenbourg's "History of Palestine," "Geikie's Christ," and a hundred other recent books, show that this is so. For the study of the relations of Christianity to the history, social order, and philosophy of the Roman Empire, which is the subject of the critical study of the Epistles, such books in popular circulation as Merivale's, Dezobry's, and Lecky's "History of Morals," are enough to show that that study is to-day a study as fresh and as important as it ever was.

Lastly, with regard to ethics or morals, no intelligent or high-minded young gentleman will enter into any discussion with me. It will be acknowledged, on all hands, to be the most vital and suggestive subject of our familiar thought and conversation.

7

Thus much reason have I for saying that a theological seminary, so far from confining itself to obsolete subjects of study, addresses itself to the most important and vital subjects of the day, if it is true to its position; nay, must do so, from the very law of its being. And thus much reason have I for saying that such a school, instead of pursuing certain antiquated methods, such as would be called functional, is in fact at this moment the only school we have of philosophy proper, speaking in distinction from that study of smoke and dust which is now called natural philosophy or science, to which we owe the present enthusiasm for what are called scientific schools.

Now, in reply to this statement, I expect to be told that the theological schools of the country are not true to their position. I shall be told at this point that what I have said is an account of what they ought to be, but that in fact they are something very different; that their professors do not dare enter freely into the popular questions of the day; and the students do not dare take them up without the countenance of the professors.

It is here, therefore, that I have to say that all that I have written I have written with the constant use of the programme of one of the oldest and best seminaries in this country,— that at Cambridge. I have no reason to doubt that many other schools can say what I say distinctly of this, from its printed reports and from official opportunities of visit and information. This school is under the nominal government of the Corporation of Harvard College; in fact, its arrangements are made by its own Faculty, who are, —

Dr. Oliver Stearns, as well known West as East.

Dr. Frederic H. Hedge, the author of "Hebrew Tradition," "Reason in Religion," "The Collection of German Prose Writers," and so many other books.

Dr. James Freeman Clarke, author among other books, of "The Ten Great Religions of the World," "The Steps of Belief," "The Truths and Errors of Orthodoxy."

Dr. Charles Carroll Everett, author of "The Science of Thought," to which I have alluded.

Prof. Edward James Young, one of our most successful students in Germany as in America.

Besides these, Prof. Sophocles, the author of "The Byzantine Dictionary;" Prof. Abbot, the American editor of Smith's "Bible Dictionary;" and several Boston clergymen, — lecture in the school.

Now, will anybody pretend to say that gentlemen who have in print and before the world used the free, broad, and scientific system which all of these gentlemen have illustrated, will, in their relations with a few students, be narrow, functional, bigoted, or petty? Can such words in any fashion be applied to such men? Can any reason be conceived why they should not do their best to make the study they have in hand broad, natural, suggestive, and even with the times? I am convinced that if any young man who believes in study which is study, will inquire of any student like himself in that, who is now in the Cambridge Divinity school, he will be told that the studies there pursued are in fact pursued in the broadest, most generous, and philosophical spirit. Nor have I any reason to say that the same may not be asserted of the other leading theological seminaries in the country.

There remains to be examined the familiar statement which we placed first, that, on entering a theological seminary, a young man pledges himself in advance to certain opinions of which he is yet to examine the foundations.

This charge, however true it may have been of other eras of the Church, is not in any sense true of the Divinity School at Cambridge; and I suppose it to be equally untrue of other leading theological seminaries. Of course, if a man is not a Christian, he will not wish to enter on a course of studies which are arranged to train him to be an effective Christian minister. The presumption is, undoubtedly, that men who study theology in Christian theological seminaries will try their abilities in the Christian ministry. But even to this they are not pledged at Cambridge. I doubt if they are so pledged at any institution of the first rank. Undoubtedly, before a young man accepts the flattering help of what are called " beneficiary funds," he should inquire very carefully what are the relations in which the acceptance of such funds involve him. They belong to a system wholly un-American, and which has no parallel in any thing else in our social order. But I can conceive of cases where the use of such funds shall imply no pledge as to the after-course of the man who uses them. And, however that may be, the entrance into a first-class theological seminary in itself, and the use of its advantages, involve no compromise of opinion whatever. At Cambridge, any man who can pass the simple literary examination, and is of good moral character, may enter. Any man who passes the regular term-examinations, and retains his moral character, may graduate, whatever his theological opinions. If he have been well prepared for entrance, and have used his three years to advantage, he may take the degree of Bachelor of Divinity; and this degree is open to him, whatever his theological convictions. Chunder Sen could take it, or Pio Nono, if they could pass, as I suppose they both could, the examinations.

There remains the question, whether the profession of the Christian ministry is worth the three years' preparation, supposing that a man find in the course of that time that he can fit himself for it respectably. Thus far I have intentionally avoided this question. I have regarded the theological seminary as what it is, — the one professional school which enlarges and continues the range of philosophical and speculative studies in which, at college, a young man begins. Neither of the other schools professes to do this. They profess to select a single walk of life, — law, medicine, physics, or engineering, and to prepare for that; but a theological school is different. Because God rules every thing, all law in whatever line, moral, physical, or historical, may be studied there; and where the school is rightly organized, it is studied there. A theological seminary, therefore, takes up and enlarges the line of study in the college.

Now, I will frankly meet the question regarding the interest or value of the ministry itself to a man choosing his profession in our time. The popular idea of the life of a clergyman is that he spends his mornings in writing sermons and translating Hebrew, and his afternoons in visiting sick people and burying the dead. The supposition is that he does all this in a certain pre-ordained or conventional way, which leaves very little play for imagination, fancy, personal character, or indeed for the intellect in any of its enterprises. As this is the popular idea, it probably enters largely into the discussions of such a club of seniors as I have imagined looking forward upon their profession. Now I confess that if young men, with the enthusiasm, vitality, and ambition of young men, liked any such life as that, or could be largely bought into it by the bribes of any education societies, I should think very sadly of our times. I believe it is because young men believe in action, advance, and in the improvement of society, that in general they reject the proposals made to them to enter such a profession, about which, for one or another reason, there hangs such a reputation. And I believe that the bounties paid by the education societies have clouded the matter more, and made it worse than before.

In point of fact, and as I observe society, this description of the life of an American clergyman is ridiculously untrue. Perhaps it would be better if a few more of them did study their Hebrew in the morning. Certainly the number that do may be counted on the fingers of a man's hands. It would not be fair, perhaps, to ask as to the private life of Bishop Simpson, Phillips Brooks, Bishop Huntington, or Dr. Bellows; but I am disposed to believe that there are few more active men in the community. As for general influence on the public, I must say that the one thing certain at school meetings, college meetings, Indian meetings, meetings to welcome and meetings to say farewell, natural-history meetings, public-library meetings, or meetings of whatever sort which have our enlarging civilization in hand, — is that the men you will meet are clergymen. Nor is the domain of literature to be forgotten. It is not by accident that, among the few first-class names in our literary history, the names of such leaders as Channing, Everett, Sparks, Bancroft, Emerson, and Ripley should be the names of

7*

clergymen. There is but one profession which of necessity trains men to express themselves simply, distinctly, and from conviction; and that profession was theirs. And if any man asks the question of general influence on men, I should be glad to be told what man at the bar, in medicine, or in any walk of physical science to-day, meets so many men directly or indirectly in America, whom he may attempt to move by personal appeal in print, or by the influence of those on whom he acts, as do the great preachers or ministers, — such men as Dr. Bacon, Bishop Simpson, Dr. Bellows, Henry Ward Beecher, or Edwin Hubbell Chapin? .

The theological seminary which shall first devise a method of showing to its students, in their vacations from the study of books and of ideas, the romantic and exciting detail of the life of a working minister; the seminary which will give them what the best medical schools do in giving a *clinique* to their students, — will, as I believe, become the most popular of professional schools, if only its conductors remember that, for the study of truth, the first requisite is freedom.

## VI.

## CHARACTER.

NO study is more impressive than the study of monuments ; or of dictionaries of biography, which in their way are monuments. As you ride into Palmyra, you pass for miles on the right and left the bases of lost statues. On these bases are carved the names of the men who were represented there. But the names do not preserve the memory of those men, more than the broken statues. The men were to be forgotten, and they are forgotten.

On the other hand Zenobia, Queen of Palmyra, has a name that lives. Longinus, one of her ministers, has a name that lives. There are no statues of Zenobia in Palmyra, — none of Longinus. But, with or without statues, they live, because there was something in them of the living sort. They were made to live.

These miles of statues were reared to the Captains of Caravans who had taken Roman gentlemen safely and cómfortably across the desert. We all know how much attached we become to a captain of a steamship, who has brought us over well. In the old days of sailing vessels and long passages to and from Europe, a frequent custom and a grateful one, indeed, was for the passengers to subscribe for a piece of silver plate for the captain who had served them. It seems that in those older days of Palmyra there was a similar habit. I suppose that, when the last day of the tedious caravan journey came, some active, busy traveller, who had no family to attend to, bustled round with a subscription paper, and made up a purse for a statue of the commander. Then a good artist was found in Palmyra, and one more statue was added to the long line of fame.

There is a like story of the decline of Athens. Athens ordered that three hundred and sixty statues should be erected to Demetrius Phalereus, one of the popular rulers of that time. But three hundred and sixty statues have not saved his name from forgetfulness. In contrast with that, as Nepos says, Miltiades, who saved

Athens from the Turk of his day, will always be remembered, — though the monument to him was only a poor water-color, which soon faded, on a temple-wall.

These stories are good enough illustrations of the eternal law, — that character is the only permanent reality in human life ; and that we cannot substitute brass or marble, not granite nor gold as a substitute. It may happen that a monument, like Cleopatra's needle, takes a name which the steadfast memory of men gives to it, in the place of the forgotten inscription once carved on its corner-stone. By the same law, they tell you at Kenilworth that Cromwell destroyed Lord Leicester's Castle. All the personal actors in its destruction are forgotten ; but Cromwell is of the type of men who live.

Literary men are for ever trying to rake out of the ashes of the past some old bit of badly melted slag, and telling us that it is good coal, or perhaps diamond, and that it should not be forgotten. Every now and then somebody tries to write up Abelard in this way. A few years ago, an accomplished scholar here tried to galvanize Charles the Bold, and make him live. But the poor corpses will not stand up long enough for men to apply the batteries which should make them twitch and start. There is nothing to live.

It is of no great consequence whether men are remembered or forgotten. But this persistency of character, in its hold on the memory of men, — if they have once found out that there is a character to remember, — is a good illustration of the absolute or eternal force of character, and the steady and certain victory which it commands. At the moment men never understand it. The town cannot understand why Charles, whom it thinks dull, moves steadily forward, while George, whom it thought brilliant, is more and more certainly set on one side. But the reason is that George is only brilliant, while Charles had the weight and force of character. In my early life, I was so placed at one time, in the discharge of my daily duty, as to be completely dependent, for two or three hours perhaps of each day, on the will or whim of two public functionaries. The superior in rank of these two was a man of unswerving truth and honor, who was however lonely, low-toned, low-spirited, probably selfish, certainly unsympathizing. The result or combination of these qualities made him what we familiarly call " cross " to everybody who came in his way. Many a day have I lost my dinner, and sunk hours of useless life, because this man would not pass a sheet of paper across his desk for me to copy, until his own work was fully done, and his own later dinner-hour come. The younger of these two men, his inferior in rank, was also a man of unswerving truth and honor, of whom then I knew little but that he was quick, sympathetic, unselfish, and kind. He did his own work well, was glad to see others do theirs well ; had exactly the same kind of work to do that the other had, but always helped us boys along ; taught us if we needed teaching, was willing to help us if the State took no peril, and won, of course, our enthusiastic love.

This man rapidly rose up the steps of our social system, received, one after another, the highest honors which this State has to give to a man in his profession, and died, only too young for us, having attained a name which will long be remembered in the walk of life to which his life was given. The other, at the first overturn in politics, lost his place; so did his junior. But my cross friend never regained his, nor indeed any position of trust. Not he. " I care for nobody, no, not I; and nobody cares for me." That is the law of such men. I used to meet him in the street, every year or two, as I grew older and older. He looked every time rather more sour and rather more hard than the time before. I am perfectly sure that all this time he was satisfying himself that the world was an unjust world and a very hard world. I do not know, but I think, that the wolf came nearer to his door and nearer with every year. And when, after twenty or more years, I read the record of his death also in the newspaper, I felt sadly sure that the grave had closed over a man who was only too willing to go ; and who died, saying that the world had not treated him fairly.

Well, I do not say that the world is a just

world, nor that time can be always relied upon
for a verdict. It is the kingdom of heaven
which is the kingdom of justice; and only
eternity can be relied upon for the truth. But
I do say that I believe that in this case of those
two men the verdict was substantially a just
verdict; and that one of them was rewarded
and the other punished because of differences
of character, which were wholly within their
own control. Yet it may be that neither of
those men was aware of the character which he
himself bore.

For character is very different from reputation, though we mix the names so often. The
English servant who wants a place, advertises
that he has a three years' character: meaning
that he has three years' reputation since anybody has known him who is willing to testify
for him, or since he lost his good reputation in
some tavern or some brawl. But though he
talks of a three-years' "character," his real
character has been forming since he drew his
first breath. The great trip-hammer of the
mint of God hits us hard, and hits us again

and hits us again; and, with every blow, the metal struck changes its lustre, changes its strength, even, changes the image and the superscription. The word character is true still to its derivation. It is a Greek word, wholly unchanged, which the Greeks derived from the word which we pronounce *harass*, which they pronounced *charass* ($\chi\alpha\rho\acute{\alpha}\sigma\sigma\omega$), but which had the meaning then that it has now. They spoke then of a coin in the mint, which was hammered and tortured by the sharp edges of the die, as being stamped upon indeed, as a poor *charassed* thing, — as bearing a character. Its *character* came to it because it was beaten, pounded by this tremendous hammer. The more it was beaten, the more distinct character it had. I believe all our words of similar import have a similar derivation. Thus, when we say a man is of this "type" of manhood, or that "type" of manhood, the original meaning is that he has been beaten into that shape by the blows of life which have passed over him. And it is true that a man's character begins when he is born, and changes or does not change accordingly as he bears the pounding which life gives him. Burns says "The rank is but the guinea's stamp." This means, at bottom, that a "pound" is metal which has been pounded. And there are metals which improve in quality all the time you stamp and hammer them. Just the same is true of man, if he have the true heat, the true life, and make himself master of the circumstance instead of slave. Precisely, now, as you may have seen different strands of iron wire brought together in a bloom, heated red, and struck and struck under a trip-hammer till they are made one, so all the different experiences of life, — the lessons, for instance, which these papers are trying to set in order, — are fused and welded into one in the process of the formation of character. A man's habits of sleep, of exercise, and of appetite ; his methods of reasoning, imagination, and memory ; his faith, his hope, his love, — are blended together in his character. And the hammering becomes no unimportant part of the process.

Certain traits of character there are which show themselves all through the pounding.

Thus, all the hammering of eternity will not make iron into gold. But a very little hammering will make pig-iron into wrought-iron, if you give it heat enough; and, so hammered, it will bear a very different strain.

I remember a lovely friend, who passed into heaven with less change perhaps than any other angel I ever saw pass from world to world. I remember she told me of a surprise of hers which exactly illustrates the permanency of some traits of character. But that life illustrates as well the change which on such traits is effected.

When she was twenty years old, her second mother called her and said: "You will like to see yourself as you were when I knew you first, a girl of six." So her mother put into her hands the letter which contained a descriptive catalogue of her faults and her merits, when, at six years old, the aunts who had trained her transferred her to this mother's care. The young woman read this early description with amazement. "I found there, in black and white," she said, "traits of mine which *I* knew very well, but which, like an ostrich, I had been carefully concealing all my life, and which I supposed no one had ever noted except myself."

All of us, perhaps, have had like experience, whether of inherited traits or of other predispositions, which, showing themselves early, crop out all along the course of life, and are among the constants which are to be managed by a man's own will. And, as this same friend of mine found out, all the interest of life, and all its value, is in the managing them and shaping them. Character is the combined work of God and man in the minting. I may, indeed, keep to the same illustration of the Greeks, of the bar of iron. It is smelted and beaten, smelted and beaten again; heated and drawn, heated and drawn again; heated and cooled suddenly, heated and cooled slowly; heated, beaten, and cooled in every conceivable way, — till, in the shape of the hair-spring of my watch, or of the needle with which you sew, or of the index in the mariner's compass, it has properties and values wholly inconceivable to the man who only knew the crude lump of pig-iron. Who

has been the actor there? The intelligent engineer, you say, who built the furnace and
brought to it the charcoal and the fluxes; who
tamed the waterfall, and set in motion the gi-
gantic wheels, and taught these trip-hammers
to move, — now with a crashing blow; now
with so slight a movement that I can gently
crack an egg-shell with it, and yet it shall not
lose its form. Yes, the engineer is one of the
actors. He is, if you please, the principal actor.
But he is not the only actor. He needs, and
therefore he has trained and has placed here,
that quiet, brave, modest, swarthy workman,
whom you see waiting by the furnace for the
hot bloom of iron to be white; who, at the fit
moment, will seize it and slide it to its place
under the trip-hammer; who then will fix it
there, that it shall profit by the blow; who will
turn it from side to side that it shall be squarely
shaped; and who, when fit moment comes, shall
cool it in the water which has been prepared.
You say he is only a day-laborer. That is true.
You say he is ignorant, unskilled in the great
powers of the universe, and could never have

set in order this giant system of which he is a part. That is true. But he is *a part* of it, all the same, and an essential part. The engineer placed him here to do this duty, and relied on his courage and conduct and fortitude, and on his original thought and discretion, that it might be done well. Nay, the engineer trained him, called out his hidden powers, and made him partner in his undertaking. Yes; and the workman has implicit faith in the mill, and in him that runs it, — risks his life on that faith; and because he trusts to the waterfall, to the furnace, and to the directing skill that sets the whole in order, he is what he is, and aids in the triumph of the whole. But for that man, ignorant and weak though he be, the bloom of iron would never become tough bar, elastic sword-blade, or prophetic needle. Place it under the trip-hammer and let this man leave it for twenty seconds, and then see how little " character " it gains, though the iron mill go steadily forward in its preordained career.

That interaction of the humble workman with the directing engineer is a fit enough representation of the interaction with God of man or woman, who are his little children, — fellow-laborers with him in this tempering and purifying and stamping which makes up " character." God does not foreordain it.   He is too kind for that. We cannot create it, we are too short-sighted for that.   But God working in us, and we working with him; in summer days of loveliness, in the night struggles of winter horror;  in the long brooding of wakeful nights, when he is the only companion ; or in that exquisite intimacy with her the dearest or with him the strongest, which is the choicest gift of a God of love, — God with his children and his children with him, year in, year out, in boyhood, girlhood, manhood, womanhood, they form together the character which seems such a mystery.

There is no adequate science of human life, which does not fitly place and fitly state this interaction of the two free agents who direct it. The life of a man differs from the life of the palm tree, or of the branching coral, precisely in this distinction, — that the man may or may not " accept the universe."   He is free to work with God if he chooses, or to oppose him if he can. According as he works with him, or as he works against him, is his success or his failure in the regular formation of his character.

Hiram Withington, a friend of my youth, whom we lost in the freshness of his promise, said the regularity or the irregularity of this formation was typified in the stratification of the great coal regions of the world. He said that every word of our lips, every act of our hands, every step of our feet, every thought of our brain, every emotion of our heart, and every vision of our fancy might be looked upon as so many dancing leaves in an autumn wind, tossed hither, tossed thither, rising now, floating then, but in the end all falling to the ground, all soaked together in a cold, clammy mass, by the dews and rains of successive night-falls; all melted together at last in the heats of trial, and crowded together under the pressure of adversity, and cooled together in winters of desolation, till in the end they made the rock which we call character. We speak of character as if it were solid and uniform, but in truth it is all

8

seamed and layered by these traces of our old
life ; and one has only to tap the rock here or
there, or where he will, and the thin strata will
lie open as if it were only yesterday that they
were crowded together ; and you shall find the
fibres and tissues, nay, you shall find the micro-
scopic cell and the fine down of the leaf, as if it
were only yesterday that it had fallen. Each
vision, each emotion, each thought, each step,
each act, and each word thus combine in the
necessary processes of human life to make up
the rock which we call character.

Now, it is according to the worth and might
of this character that the man or woman succeeds or fails. Let me return to my cross
and gentle masters, of whom I have spoken
already. For here is what men and women are
always forgetting ; what both of them, perhaps,
forget. If the character is light and trivial, no
matter how elegant the accomplishment nor how
ingenious the tool of one's labor. So there be
no might and force behind, tool and accomplishment are flung away ; and, as human lives are
tested by whatever fire or whatever flood, the

revelation which is made, and cannot be escaped, is a revelation of how much might and force and strength of character there is in the man. Pathetic enough is it to see this in any moment of history. In Queen Anne's time, for instance, a hundred and seventy years ago in England, there were noblemen and noble-women, court beauties, court jesters, and court gallants in London; there were politicians working for the queen, and politicians working against her; there were actors and actresses who were the talk and toast of all England, poets and other writers who were libelling each other, libelling half the people in the land, and not forgetting to libel the crown. In the midst of them all was Isaac Newton, whom every one respected; yes, but neither courtier, actor, poet, nor satirist knew that his work, his power, and so his name would outlive them all. The prime minister rode to his office, and flattered himself that Newton was specially gratified when his lordship recognized him as he passed in at the office door, — Newton being master of the mint. To give a man an appointment in the mint was the only way in

which Government could acknowledge, what
the Government knew, that here was the great
thinker, great scholar, great man of the time.
Well, time rolls by, and we find what was what.
First, the memory of the actors' and the actresses' paint and powder die. Then dies the
memory of the trashy plays they acted. Then
dies the memory of the intrigues of the men of
party. Treaty of this,. treaty of that; Marl-
borough's victories, Bolingbroke's lies, — we have
forgotten them all. By and by the books are remembered only as names in literature. Persons
of tact who know they ought to have them in
their libraries are tempted to make the sets out
of wood with well-gilt leather covers. Of Mr.
Pope, a man of true genius, by far the most
brilliant author of them all, a Harvard graduate said the other day to Mr. Fields, as they
looked upon his portrait, "Were you acquainted
with Mr. Pope, Mr. Fields?" So the fire of time
tries these reputations. So the straw burns,
the stubble, the lath, and the rafter; the stucco
and plaster crumble and give way. But in
the midst of it something remains: it is the

work which stands for character, and represents
character. The work of Newton stands unchanged : his name too may be forgotten, but his
work is here. He helped men one step nearer
to their God. He brought in Law where all
was lawless. He did this, he said, by untiring
industry and determined perseverance, not by
any flash of brilliant inspiration. On the strand
of the Eternal Ocean he picked up a few pebbles, and these pebbles are as truly jewels of
eternal lustre as they ever were.

> " Nature and Nature's Law lay hid in night —
> God said 'Let Newton be,' and all was light."

This is what one of those brilliant wits of his
own time said of him, and said truly. And that
service rendered by faith and courage to human-
ity stands, and will stand. His name may be
forgotten like the rest. But in the higher certainty of truth, in the nearer walk with God, in
the clearer significance of Law, are testimonies
never to be lost of the might and wealth and
worth of character. Work done for the day, by
the creatures of a day, has died with the day.
Work done for the eternities, by the eternal

powers which a child of God enlists in his service, is work as real now as it was then. The
man's name is forgotten, or it is remembered.
That is nothing. The work stands unchanged,
and the contrast is the contrast between the
worthlessness of mere accomplishment and the
value to all time of the work of character.

I think the habit of our country leads men to
forget this contrast.

True, there is not a wood-cutter in Maine or
Minnesota but knows that the weight of the axe
and the swiftness of the stroke are what tell in
the cutting of the tree; that the sharpness of
the axe is nothing unless there be weight and
swiftness behind it. There is not a man of
them who would go into the wilderness expecting to clear his farm with sharp-bladed pen-
knives or well-polished scissors. Yet the same
men, as they look round for their heroes, as
they give applause or as they give votes, are as
likely as any men to be misled by the brilliancy
of accomplishment, and to forget the necessity,
if the work is to last, of the weight and force
which only belong to character. I think our

habit — what was our necessity — of seeking immediate results, leads to this. As we burned down the forests, and now find too late that we have caused by our folly higher freshets in the spring and longer droughts in the summer, so we applaud some showy fool in the pulpit, or elect men to office for their ease in public speaking, to find only too late that the children do not know what the word religion means, and that the destinies of the State have not been confided to statesmen. This mistake, whenever it is committed, is the mistake of preferring accomplishment above character, — a mistake fatal whether it is made in education, in our estimate of ourselves and our plan of our duty, in our selection of other men for office, or in the verdict of praise and censure which we render to the servants of the State or of the Church.

We meet every day the broken-bladed pen-knives, — people who have tried to do the work of axes, and have failed because they had not weight enough. Such men are looking round for patrons and letters of recommendation. They think this man was successful because of his uncle's influence, and that one because he was a freemason; and then say bitter things of society because society does not help them forward. The truth is, all the while, that there is nothing to help, nothing to endorse, nothing to rely upon. The man has failed, not because he had no uncles or no endorsers, but because he had no weight, no steadfastness, no character.

And, on the other hand, I meet every day this man and that woman who cannot see why God leaves them to such petty detail in the work of his army. "Why should I be left to take care of babies, while Penthesilea can lead Amazons into action?" "Why should I be left to take a class in a Sunday-school, while at my age William Pitt was Prime Minister of England?" Why, but because the good God, who has something better at stake than the work of Amazons or of prime ministers, has devised these schools for the creation of your character. Dear boy, you did nothing all last week, in your new employ, but to add up units and carry tens, and add tens and carry hundreds; and you are sure

that you could have done so much more and so
much better, but no man asked you. Is the
new employ, for that, mere slavery to you?
Only see what is the true sum of your figures
and the true product of your multiplication.
Be sure, you, that five years hence, when somebody wants a man of might, of trust, of honor,
of·integrity, and looks for him in that crypt
where you are adding and multiplying, the
search shall not be made in vain. Show,
then, that among a thousand ciphers there
is one real value. Among a thousand names,
let there be one child of God. Show, then and
there, what the service of five faithful years can
do in creating character.

As I watch men of affairs, I find one set who,
as they say, make one hand wash another.
They are rushing round at one o'clock to pick
up the funds to pay the note which falls due
at two.

I find another set, more thoughtful, who
know to-day what they are to do next Friday, —
know, as they would say, where they shall be
next Saturday, — who are thus prepared in ad-

vance for any exigency in business. You cannot take them by surprise.

And, once more, I hear of a third set sometimes. I hear traditions of the great men of affairs, whose dealings have been governed by combinations which were years in maturing; who knew how many acres of this world were planted with coffee four years before, how many three years before, what would be the probable crop two years after, and three, and four. Such are the men not satisfied to imitate their rivals, to do as others do, to work by rule of thumb; but who have a principle, on which even commerce adjusts itself. I might say the first of these is a merchant by knack; the second, a merchant by system; the third, a merchant on principle. That familiar series illustrates for us sufficiently a gradation vastly more important, — a gradation in men's lives, related not to the laws of trade, but to the eternal realities. Men and women of accomplishment are living for the more immediate effect, and trusting the immediate effort. Men and women of mere system are only repeating what some schoolmaster or some cyclopædia suggested. But men and women of character !—ah, there we stand with those who are not satisfied with time! They are not satisfied with to-day's effort or to-day's success. Nay, they are not satisfied to know that next week this shall be adjusted, or that smoothed away. They are not satisfied till the word they speak shall ring as true as the eternal word, and the house they build be built upon the rock eternal. There is the man, there is the woman, to whom, in crisis or in calamity, friend, neighbor, country turn. There is the man, there is the woman, who in new exigency rises to the exigency; needs not to be taught what to do or how to do it, but does it as `from " native impulse, elemental force." There is the man or woman whose work stands. Their names may be forgotten. So are the names of almost all martyrs. But their lives. live in the higher life of a world renewed!

## VII.

## RESPONSIBILITIES OF YOUNG MEN.

An Address delivered in the South Congregational Church, Boston. March 22, 1874.

I HAVE tried, a hundred times, to illustrate in this place the duty of young men who go out from an old community like ours into the new States or the new Territories. In one year I parted from four such young men. I had with each of them most serious talk as to the great duty before them and the noble responsibility before them. Frederick Wadsworth Loring was one of them. There are young men here who well remember him in school, — a quick, intense boy, putting questions far in advance of his years, while he was not easily satisfied with commonplace answers, I suppose. I remember seeing him when he was but seven years old, so quick, so mature, that I despaired of his growing to manhood. But he did grow to manhood, in strong health, too, — such a mother had he and such a father, — and without the loss of any of the qualities which made his childhood admirable. Pure and affectionate, he passed through college with a literary taste and accomplishment hardly equalled at his age. He devoted himself to a life of letters ; [1] and as correspondent of one or two of our leading journals he went with one of the Government surveying parties into Arizona and California. As he was returning, strong and well, the stage coach in which he rode was attacked by Indians and he was instantly killed.

Frank Russell Firth, who was not one of our number here, but sometimes joined us in our afternoon service, the personal friend of many to whom I speak, was the first boy I knew among the pupils in the Technological School. He distinguished himself there as he did everywhere, and graduated in their first

---

[1] Beside articles in different journals, Mr. Loring published "Two College Friends," Boston, 1871. He made the plan for "Six of One and Half a Dozen of the Other," and contributed two poems to it. Many of his poems are in "Poetry of the Advocate;" and a volume of them was published in 1871.

class in 1868. He looked round for his place in the world, as all young men have to, and as they all wonder that they have to ; was never discouraged, used every moment wisely and well, and, when he was hardly of age, was in charge of an important railroad line in Kansas and Nebraska. On a tour of inspection, he stationed himself on the front of the engine of his train, that he might note rightly the deflection of a bridge which they were to pass. The bridge gave way, and Frank Firth was crushed under the engine. He lived scarcely long enough to see his father, and to bid his friends good-by.

With him at the moment was Otis Everett Allen, also known to many of you. He had just graduated at Harvard College, the honored son of an honored father, one of my near friends. His father died just as he entered college, and this boy was loyally entering on life in the manly wish to do for his mother and his sister what man might do. Between him and Firth there was an attachment as of the heroes of romance. He had joined him on his perilous post of duty, and died instantly in the same fatal fall.

Of these two young men a little biography has been published this winter, well worthy the careful reading of every boy who hears me, and who is old enough to be asking himself what is to be his place in life.[1] I have read it myself again and again, and I have perhaps learned as much from it as from any book, as to the question what our first-rate schools do for the first-rate boys who go to them, and what the first-rate boys mean to do for the world. I associate these three lives and these three deaths, indissolubly with the life and death of a fourth young man, — much better known to you than any of these of whom I have spoken.

George Gilman Chapin was the first boy whom I baptized in the public service of this church. I have never forgotten the manly way in which he came to me, at his father's side, nor the modesty and intelligence of his nature, — which showed even then, when I supposed he was not nine years old, that his interest in the whole service was devout and real. It was impossible

[1] "The Young Engineer." A Memoir of Frank Russell Firth. With a sketch of the Life of Otis Everett Allen. Boston: 1874.

not to be interested in such a boy; and never in after life did he fail to make good the bright omen of that morning in Whitsuntide.

He entered Harvard College, and worked there with distinction, but left before graduating. He was the practical and efficient secretary of our Young People's Society here, ready to lend a hand wherever he could be of service. It was but a little after Firth and Allen died, that I met him in St. Paul in Minnesota, where he had established himself, and where everybody honored him and respected him. I was with him a great deal while I was there. There never was a more beautiful instance of the way in which a conscientious and highly-trained young man could carry to a new community just what a new community needs. I was proud of him and of all that he was doing. And then, that curtain dropped too. A little while after, and he died almost as suddenly as the others, from a violent typhoid fever. I had seen him, as it seemed, for the last time.

One may well compare such losses in the great investment which we are all the time mak-

ing, for the building up of our country, with the
losses of the Civil War. Death did not come
then more often, more sadly, nor more suddenly,
when our brave boys went to battle as frankly
and as willingly as you boys go to a ball or to the
play. To us who are left, it is no little lesson
which we learn when such deaths arrest our
attention, if we can see how important is the
place which young men hold in social order.
While such men live, we are looking forward
to their future. It is when they die, we look
back and begin to count their worth.

And I observe, as I know you young men
observe, that in new communities the value
of the element of young life is apprehended.
When you read of the traditions of New England, you will find that such or such a man, the
founder of a town, heard of a good man at some
settlement, and rode down there to see if he
could not secure him. He would know that his
town could not thrive without men, and so he
would go down and offer such a homestead,
such a mowing lot, such a stand for a blacksmith's shop, if only the man would come.

Now, you do not see in exactly the same form that necessity now. But none the less is it true that at this hour America differs from all the rest of the world except Australia, and is for real life a better country to grow up in than the older parts of the world, because of, I think, the larger opportunities given here to young men. I am afraid that the young men of cities do not recognize this. But I have no doubt that it is true. More than once have I heard young Americans laugh as they described their first interviews with their business correspondents in London, when they noted the extreme surprise with which those elderly men found out that they had been corresponding on terms of equality with gentlemen who, when they came in person, looked, as they would say, like boys. Take our country through, there is no doubt that we have this great advantage of a new country. So long as every man may have his own farm by going and taking it, the habit or tendency of young men will be to establish themselves, instead of living in what they regard dependence. So the earlier generations here grew up, — and that principle survives. George Washington was almost the Nestor of the men with whom he advised in the war. They are always speaking of his dignity and even his venerable aspect. He was forty-three when it began. Greene, his only second, was thirty-five ; Pickering, his commissary-general, was twenty-five ; Hamilton, his favorite aid, was twenty when he was appointed to that position, and Lafayette was commissioned major-general when he was nineteen. Hancock was thirty-nine when, as president of Congress, he signed the Declaration of Independence. That sort of willingness to intrust important duty to men in young life has never died out of the country. I find that the average age of the representatives in Congress this year is forty-three years. Almost all these men must have served in their own States in trusts of importance before they came to Congress. I believe the habit is readily accounted for by reference to the requisitions on any new country. It is the habit of a frontier, of new exigencies ; and it has been and is, as I believe, to this country, a constant blessing.

Let me read you a little passage from Mr. Beecher, — which I found since I wrote this sermon, in a sermon of his which I wish you would all read, — which he calls " Manhood in America." He says: —

" The value of all men, without regard to race or condition, is the essential, democratic, American idea. The true democratic idea is that ' a man's a man for a' that,' or this or that or any thing else. The real democratic American idea is, not that a man shall be on a level with every other man, but that every man shall be what God made him, without let or hindrance; that there shall be no prejudice against him if he be high, and that no disgrace shall attach to him if he be low; that he shall have supreme possession of what he has and what he is; that he shall have liberty to use his forces in any proper direction."

Now this is as true regarding young men as it is of black men or red men, rich men or poor men. They shall have liberty to use their forces in any proper direction.

And that habit of the country ought to be

recognized by young men who have had advantages above the average in early training. Such men have to ask themselves, What is the place of young men in American life? And I do not now put that question for those who go away from us into the wilderness. There are not a few young men, let us be thankful, who remain here at home. It is the opportunities and responsibilities which come before them as young men, which occupy us to-day.

Well, they are prompt to say that theirs is not the average American lot; that promotion here is *not* rapid; that it is all as if they were in an old country. I believe this is only partly true; but if it were wholly true, it would not affect what I have to say of their duties.

The illustrations I have taken for convenience from the Revolution, are illustrations from military or political life. But I should say that the first lesson for a young man in Boston to learn, would be that, though every man has an important duty to his country, there are a thousand ways to discharge that duty without fighting for her, or going into the legislature, or trying

to do so. We are deceived here by the accidents
of present history. Probably some man is now
at work in Boston, studying over some chemical
process, or some mechanical invention, which
fifty years hence will be referred to as one of
the great social improvements of our time; as
men speak of the railroad now, or of the invention of the sewing-machine, or of Grove's and
Daniell's sustaining batteries, which made the
telegraph possible. You and I do not know
who these men are who are pushing these
researches. No! They do not try their experiments in Faneuil Hall, or on the Common.
And so, because the people who do try their
experiments in public, go into print, so that
you and I read about them night and morning,
we persuade ourselves, if we are foolish, that
they are the most important people of our time.
But not if we are wise — only a little wise.
For then we know that Robert Fulton did a
greater work for this country than ever James
Madison did; and that Whitney, who was the
inventor of the cotton gin, did more to establish
American wealth and the prosperity of the

Southern States than all the Southern orators
and statesmen of his time or of all time put
together.

I. The first lesson of any man, I should say,
must be that he must serve his kind, — and of
course his country, — but that this is to be in
the line of his own genius. That phrase is Mr.
Emerson's ; and if a man do not know what is
the line of his own genius, as most of us do not
know, let a man be sure that whatever advantages he has gained in boyhood anywhere be
steadily improved upon. For God reigns ; and
it is as sure as that, that God will call, even to
the front, every child of his who has any service
to render. The standing difficulty in the long
run is not want of places, but want of men.
You find it very hard to believe this now, when
you see every advertisement for a clerk answered
by two hundred applicants. But once go behind the scenes of practical life, — once hear
the careful inquiry made by men of large under-
takings and large results, where they can find
men of large capacity, or men of absolute hon-

esty, or men of hard perseverance, or even men who, being well up in their specialty, neither drink nor lie nor steal, — and you will understand what I·mean when I say the need, on the whole, is the need of men. You will see a man is bound in honor to improve the ability he has while he can improve it, and to be ready for the exigency which it is certain will come. It comes sooner to one man than to another. Yes: it comes to one man in the demands of a great invention. It comes to another man because there is a new necessity in literature. It comes to another man in some new arrangement of government. It comes to another man because he proves to be a born apostle of some lesson in the Gospel not before wrought out sufficiently. It comes to another man in the horrors of civil war. It comes in different ways, but to each man it comes. I do not say fame comes, nor money, nor comfort, nor happiness; but I say that such is the blessing of an eager young country like ours, which lives a century in every year, that opportunity comes to every man; opportunity to serve mankind and so to serve

God; opportunity to make two blades of grass grow somewhere where only one blade grew before; opportunity to leave the world a better world than he found it.

II. But woe to the man who is not ready for the opportunity when it comes! Here is the pith and point of the parable which describes the mysterious coming of the Son of God, and tells how some are ready for the wedding, and some have their wicks burned dry and their lamps empty. In that is just the difference between the man who, when there is something to do, is eager to try to do it, and the other man, who is not all a man, who is not ready, and knows he must let the moment go by. The old symbolic image of Time had that one forelock on the forehead, and one must catch at that or he could catch nowhere. And, as we say every day, in this country of ours, and in our civilization, "Time moves more quickly than he ever did before." That is true. And a man needs to be more ready than ever before to be of use when his moment does appear. And this is certain, that he will not find his opportunity by sitting in the reading-room of a hotel, with his feet upon the window-seat, looking out into the street, and seeing if the opportunity will ride up the street or ride down. I do not think that he will find his opportunity by going to ward meetings, arranging that William shall be chosen overseer of the poor, and John be chosen school-committee man. I hope he will go to the ward caucus, but I hope he will not expect to find his opportunity in life there. No; his opportunity to serve the world comes as he improves his own ability; and, speaking generally, this is to be his ability in the walk of life in which he is.

Is he a manufacturer? Let him know to the bottom the chemistry, the history, and the combination of the articles he makes. Let him some day make them better. Is he a merchant? Let him, at the end of this month, know something about his own line of goods that he did not know when the month began. Is he a man of letters? Let him fill up faster than he pumps out from the cistern. The man who is always enlarging what is after all a man's real capital, need not be afraid to meet the world fairly.

Or it may be, of course, that it is not in a man's vocation but in his avocation that he is at work, getting ready to be of more service. And I have no doubt that every man should have a regular avocation as well as a vocation, were it only for that physical relief of which Brown-Sequard has been teaching us. So George Livermore retired every day from his business — I suppose I may say at the head of the wholesale wool merchants of this city — and in his peerless library made himself the leader in the lines of delicate and difficult critical study which he selected. So Nathaniel Bowditch retired regularly from his duty in the life office, and gave a fixed time to the translation of La Place's "Mécanique Céleste." So Benjamin Franklin retired from the supervision of the best printing-office in America, to make the electrical experiments and discoveries which in that line changed the science of the world. I select, as my instances, Boston men, intentionally. From my limited acquaintance here, I could name a hundred men who are doing something of just that sort now, in lines which seem to me not less important than these which I have named. But I do not think it right to speak of living men. And what I want to do is to try to state the principle upon which they are all working.

They are determined that they will be more fit to serve the king next year than they are now. That is the whole story. They did not "finish their education" when they left the High School, or the Dwight School, or Harvard College. All of them have found a post-graduate course that they can work in. For they have found out, all of them, that they are children of God, and, as children of God, bound to help forward somewhere in God's world.

I hear with utter satisfaction, then — satisfaction with which nothing else compares — that any two or three of my young friends have made a little club together to study chemistry or electricity, or Italian or French, or Shakspeare or Chaucer, or butterflies or beetles, or botany or geology (if it be really study); to read "The Science of Thought," or the "Provençal," or the "Laocoön." To know that two or three young people have covenanted and agreed together that they will be worth more six months hence than they are to-day, — it involves almost every thing so far as they are concerned. These studies themselves are not to be spoken of as trifling. Limit the subjects resolutely, bind each other to loyal work, and you have opportunities for really important results, leading farther than you know, or I. But it is not for mere results that I am anxious, or am forelooking. It is for those who form such clubs that I speak. They gain the mutual help, which is so much. There is so much less danger that they will take the hand from the plough. And when you really see, in a fair instance, that such a combination has been bravely and faithfully maintained, you may almost say that you are sure that God will find there faithful servants; and that, when the bell strikes, there will be among them those who can do the duty and bear the burden which in his counsels are imposed.

Nor does this which I am saying require or
imply that the man I am talking about is to give
himself up to books after a day's work in some
confined employment. He may do that, or he
may not. The point is simply that somehow
and somewhere he is to enlarge his working
power. One man does this, as Frederic Turell
Gray did it, by devoting his off-time to the poor
around him, — a study which with him went so
far, that from the movements set on foot by him
and others like him grew up the whole system
of the Benevolent Fraternity of churches here.
As he and those men saw that system, and
looked forward to its development, it looked
forward to a real spiritual oversight of this
whole city, — of every exile in it, every stranger,
every lonely man or woman.

That is the work of a young publisher, who
took this as his avocation. Some men do it in
perfecting a new invention. Some men do it
by making life tolerable to exiles who have no
friend but those who seek them half way.
" How in the world did a busy man like you
learn the Hungarian language?" said I to a

partner in one of the largest business firms in the world. " Oh," said he, " there was a poor dog of a Hungarian officer, who was starving in an attic, and I found it comforted him to have me come and talk with him; and it ended in our reading Hamlet together in the Hungarian version." So, when the bell struck, that man was ready to use the language which by what you please to call accident he had learned. I know a man who learned the Spanish language from the barber who shaved him; and he told me that the knowledge was, as it proved, of essential service to him and to other men in all his after life. A young lady came to me once, complaining of the sad want of good society in the manufacturing town of forty thousand people in which she lived. I told her she did not know where to seek it. I lived in another manufacturing town of half that population; and I told her that the only nobleman I had ever known, of absolutely blue blood of sixteen quarterings, — a man whose ancestors were noble before Columbus guessed at America, — was a man whose acquaintance I made when he came to my front door and asked if I had an old coat that I could give him. An accomplished gentleman he was, too, — temperate, honorable, and manly. But he was an exile, and in overwork for his daily bread he had become blind. Take these as instances of the ways wholly outside of closet study, in which a man may be gaining new resources and growing more ready for the duty to which it may please God to call him.

And of such detail I must say no more. My object, indeed, was not to speak of detail. My object was to warn young men against the mistake which the French and English books are a little apt to inculcate, — the mistake of supposing that it is of no great consequence where or how a man spends the years from twenty to thirty. It is of infinite consequence. To us in America, in every step in social order, in every physical impediment, in every political revolution, it is of visible, palpable importance, if a man will only put out his fingers to feel, or open his eyes to see. We live among revolutions. Tremendous things are happening all the time. It is the Boston fire. It is the September panic. It is the destruction of Chicago. · It is the Civil War. It is an inundation in Louisiana. Or, such convulsions apart, we live a life of surprises. A city doubles its population in a dozen years. The whole line of its business changes in twenty. A new current of emigration sets in here. A new line of exports opens there. All this means that America, while it is America and because it is America, needs all the time new men and young men. It needs that these young men shall be ready.

And that readiness is not to be the alacrity of the fencing-master, the deportment of the manners-master, the selfishness of a Pelham, or the etiquette of a Chesterfield. It is to be the manliness of a man. Here is one more child of God. He is a child who, when he became old enough to see and to hear, opened his eyes that they might see, his ears that they might hear, — yes, and his heart that it might understand. Of his own manly free will he determined to be "partaker of the divine nature." That is something more than to be a rival of Chesterfield, or a disciple of Turveydrop. To be a "partaker of the divine nature;" to be as true as God himself; as loving to those in need as God's Son well beloved; as ready to serve as the loyal child should be to the Father who never fails. This child of God thus determining, thanks God first, last, always, that he has placed him in a society where each can lend a hand, and where no man gainsays his endeavor. Proud of the ancestry who have given to him such privileges, he is determined that to his children these privileges shall go down. Then to the exiles from other lands, who did not inherit such privileges, he is determined that, in their own despite, they shall transmit them to their children! Yes; and he sees and knows and understands where is the central life of all such endeavor. That life came into the world when the great password was spoken: "Bear ye one another's burdens." That life began for the world· when, in the greatest epoch of its life, the world found that it was one world, — of one heart and of one soul. It began when men began to live each for each in infinite attraction, and secluded themselves no longer each alone in beastly separation. He knows the law of this new life. He knows the history of this new life. And to the reunited world, the world redeemed in it ; to the universal Church, the kingdom of its God — he consecrates his life and his endeavor : life and endeavor never so noble or so beautiful as when they are offered by the young knight just as he is admitted to knighthood, and laid, as the first fruits of his manhood, upon the altar of his God!

## VIII.

## STUDY OUTSIDE SCHOOL.

I HAVE just returned from a visit to Antioch College, — an institution established by the Unitarian church, near a quarter of a century ago, for the higher education of the young people of this country, — especially in the Middle States. I have for some years held the post of chairman of the Trustees of the funds collected for this purpose. It is, therefore, my official duty to attend once a year at its commencement.

There is something very interesting, pathetic indeed, in the start upon life thus made at such a time by high-strung, well-taught young people, — quite sure that they are to conquer the world; and there is something very sweet in the sympathy and confidence with which the hopes of the graduates are regarded by those behind them.

Our class-day and college commencement, and the closing exercises of all the schools, are going to show us just the same thing here. And so I am going to talk to you young people about the use to be made of freedom from school and college, — in continuing the line of life and study into which school or college have introduced you.

For I suppose there is no time when a boy or girl feels the worth of school-training as they do at the moment when they leave it for ever. When the chance is over, you feel that you could have done more with it. When you see how others have improved, you wonder why you did not take the same steps as they. You pack up the elementary school books, to say, "Some-time and somehow, I will know more of these things than the elements." Nay, even if you look back with relief on the old restrictions which are done with for ever, duly grateful that for you study-bells and regular atten-dance in the class-room exist no longer, that sense of freedom suggests the resolve that the free man shall use time to more advantage than the boy found when he was thus hampered and crippled by chains and rules.

Well, I begin with saying to my young friends that the plans they form now of continuing school studies on a more generous plan, less cramped and more in unison with their tastes, are wholly justified in the resources open to them here, and in the omnipotence of their period of life, if only they will hold to the hope or plan with tolerable loyalty. Other dreams of youth may be fallible and foolish, but the determination of the boy or girl of seventeen to be through life a scholar is in no sense fallible or foolish in the conditions of society among us. No matter who or what that boy or girl may be. Printer's boy like Franklin; bound girl in a log-cabin like Mrs. Farnham; merchant's clerk like George Livermore; shoemaker's apprentice like Henry Wilson or Roger Sherman, — any one who determines at seventeen to use an hour each morning and an hour each night in systematic study, will come out at the end of twenty years among the systematic scholars of the land. They are not a large class, but they are a class of men and women happy, contented, and useful; happy and contented because useful, and useful because happy and contented.

Now I am going to speak specially, to-day, not of general training for life, but simply of these visions and hopes of school boys and school girls for keeping up mental training; I am going to speak of what I believe the best methods and the necessary cautions, as far as I can, from my own experience.

I. First of all, I am speaking of and I suppose myself speaking to young people who have regular work to do in this world besides keeping up the studies of school. My first business is to tell them that their position has distinct advantages, and that their disadvantages for study do not overweigh the advantages, — as I hope I shall show. I have, therefore, suggested that I do not expect them to give more than twelve hours a week, or two hours a day, to the regular study which I suppose them to be undertaking. This is more time than the average professional man — doctor, lawyer, clergyman, or civil engineer — gives to general systematic study.  Any such man would be glad indeed if anybody would guarantee him two hours for systematic work in general study, aside from what he has to give to the bread-and-butter work, or hand-to-mouth work, in which he takes up to-day the particular information which he needs for the particular requisition of to-morrow. Two hours a day of systematic study, if you can get it, is all that any men, but the two or three who are exceptionally favored, pretend to use for it as the year goes round.

II. With regard to the subject of reading or study, you begin now to find the advantage of leaving school.  School lays a foundation.  From the nature of the case it has to lay the same foundation for you all.  One of the wisest and wittiest women of our time once put it thus to me : —

" At school we are taught a little botany, and a little physiology, and a little chemistry, and a little natural philosophy; a little of metaphysics, and a little of morals, and a little of history; a little Latin, a little French, a little Italian, a little German and Greek; a little arithmetic, a little algebra, a little geometry, — at school we are taught a little of every thing." True enough; that is precisely what the higher schools are for. They are to give the scholar a taste. Then let him go forward if he will, where he will, and as he will. Two or three of the last years of school have not been badly spent, if they have given such a series of glimpses round the panorama that you can wisely choose which direction you will take for your own journey.

Now you have the luxury of making your own choice. And now you are to study, — not ten things at a time, but one thing. And here is one of the places where your taste, your fancy, — what you like, — may come in. The rule for gratifying one's tastes in life is exact here. You must do the duty next your hand, that is certain; but of ten duties next your hand you are to choose that which you do most happily, which suits you best, or for which God fitted you. So long as you were at school, it was your duty to do what the schoolmaster told you to do. Now, of this realm of reading or study, it is your duty to choose first that which you need most or like best. And now you are to drop the effort to follow up ten lines of study at a time. Now you are to select, for your two hours daily, some one out of the ten.

III. And you are to choose now, no longer as one playing with the elements, but as a student who is going to do this thing thoroughly.

Do not ask me to choose for you. I do not know. I cannot tell either what your tastes are or your duties. It may be that your father is an importer of drugs, that it is interesting and valuable for you and for him to know of all manner of plants, from the cedar of Lebanon to the hyssop under the wall. In that case, I should think you would study botany; and study it, not satisfied with pulling a violet to pieces to count its stamens, but so to study it as to learn the laws of growth, the territorial division of genera and species, the relations of climate to growth, and again of vegetation to climate. I should think you would like to enter into the heart and marrow of your father's daily duty, and of what you are to hear of every day of your life.

Or you may be touched by all this centennial clamor, Fourth of July jubilation, Old South preservation and the rest. I should think you would like to know something of the real history of your country beneath the school-book gloss; what manner of men Hancock and the Adamses, Quincy, Ward, Warren, and the other Massachusetts heroes really were; what Jefferson, and Paine, and Dickinson, and Schuyler, and Livingston were. I should think you would like to study a hundred years ago in the writings of a hundred years ago; in the words, I mean, of the actors, and their times.

Or in this daily talk of politics and social matters deeper than politics, I should think that a boy or girl of seventeen leaving school, might resolve boldly to understand some of the principles at the bottom of questions of hard money and soft money, of free trade and protection; of grangers, and eight-hour laws, and trade-unions.  This would be to study sociology and political economy.

Or I can understand how and why such a boy or girl, not satisfied with the smattering of Latin, or German, or French he has brought from school, should resolve to go beyond the mere elements of the language into the luxury of the literature.  Nor can any moment be more delightful than the moment when such a person at last launches loose from the ties which have bound him to the dictionary, and starts over the ocean of a great literature, unfettered and free, conquering a new world by the magic of a new language.

Choose for yourself, you who have a right to choose now ; but choose one thing first, and do not add the second till you are certain about the one.  Do not let John persuade you to study French, and Max to study German, and Henry to study astronomy, and Walter to study chemistry.  Do not think because you are free you can do every thing.  You are to do one thing at a time, if you do it well.  One thing well done, of course you may take another.

French well mastered, take your French to study chemistry. Chemical analysis well understood, use it in studying mineralogy. The mathematics of mineralogy well compassed, use it in your studies of geology. But do not be trying to compass all these things at once and together.

On the other hand, if you can find a companion to do your work with you, two of you together will achieve each twice as much as one would do alone. I do not lay much stress on the teacher. A great teacher, who will inspire you, is certainly a great blessing. But wonders can be done in the way of study by resolute learners who have no teachers. I do hope, for each of you, that you will have companionship and sympathy.

IV. And, now, one word as to the first practical difficulty you are going to meet; or, shall I say, the first enemy in your way. I have supposed that, from your household and social duties, you girls are going to win two hours for study; and that, from your daily work at the store, you boys are going to win two. The first temptation will be to give those two hours to novel-reading, to the magazines, or at the least to the newspapers and reviews, on the ground that they are improving. What are you to do about these?

Well, I have profited too much by novels to say hard things about them. I recognize absolutely the truth that the finest work of the literature of our time has taken that form. I think there is no English book of the last twenty years which has a better chance with posterity than George Eliot's novels. But when I see the trash which boys and girls have in their hands in the street cars; when I see what people buy and devour in travelling; when I see what lies about on people's tables and seashore piazzas and mountain hotels, — I know that I must speak of the worst temptation for young people let loose from school. There is no such enemy to firm and intelligent study as the unrestricted habit of devouring novels. Hold that in check, therefore, from the beginning. From the beginning, determine that for every

hour of novel reading in a day, you will read
for an hour something of some worth beside the
excitement of the hour. The old ladies who
sent to the Dorchester Public Library a half
century' ago, used to send for " a sermon-book
and another book," leaving to the librarian to
choose. I wish their granddaughters to-day,
when they. send for a novel, would send for
"another book" as well, and never would take
novel number two till the "other book" had
been well and wisely digested. The analogy of
sugar-plums is perfect. Woe to the boy or girl
who eats candy all the time ; because a little
sweetmeat has its place — and a very good
place. The solid meals of the day have their
place, too. And this is all that I will say. But
I forewarn you that, when at New Year you are
looking back on the resolutions about your
studies which you have not kept, the failure
will be, not that you have read nothing, but that
what you have read was not worth the reading.

V. Now in this whole affair the key is this:
your study is not for so poor an object as to

please yourself; it is, in the end, that you may please those you love. Yes, I have a great respect for the girl who studied chemistry so that she might the better make the sugar-plums for her younger brothers and sisters. I think her chemistry was God-favored; and I have no doubt that the spirit in which she conceived her task lifted her up all along and carried her bravely through. To be enlarging steadily the mental power God gave when you were born, that you may carry out his purpose the more steadily, may bring this world nearer heaven, — that is your object when you choose this or that direction for your reading. Or, if you choose modestly to define it in less terms, and to say you would be a better companion to your mother, or would serve better your little brothers in their studies, I will accept that definition. I only say that that means the same thing. If, in the schools, the poor vision of culture for the sake of culture has been haunting you, let us thank God that you are out of the schools; and let us pray to him that life, with its duties and dangers, may lay that ghost, and lay him for ever.

I hate the word "Culture," it has been so paraded and discussed, — the theme of platforms and of lectures that meant nothing. It has been so mixed up with conceit and selfishness that I had rather you told me any friend of mine was a woman of pleasure, or a woman of fashion, than that she was a person of "culture," as that phrase is commonly applied. An indignant Western writer the other day said that when the Chinook Indians wished to stamp a wordy pretender with their lowest contempt; when they wanted to speak of the maximum of brag with the minimum of performance; when, for instance, they would describe a young chief who had never been on the war-trail, and had never looked an enemy in the face, but who was perfect in his war-paint, carried weapons of the most elaborate make, and wore more feathers than any warrior of them all, — they described this man by the name, "Boston Cultus."

Well, you and I know what that satire means, and we know where it is deserved. It is deserved by the men who say the country is

10

going to the dogs, and who never give a vote to save it. It is deserved by the men who found fault with every movement of the war, and never carried a musket. It is deserved by the men who say the sharpest and smartest things against universal suffrage, and yet never lifted a finger to welcome an emigrant, nor spent a dollar to teach a negro. It is deserved by the men who say the West is a horde of barbarians, who yet never travelled farther west than the Saratoga race-courses, nor looked face to face at the pure democracy of a healthy Western town. Such satire is fairly enough deserved in its place ; but it has no voice against the culture which makes of Boston a university ; which fills it every winter with young men and women from every State this side of the Pacific, who have come here to study music, or language, or painting, or philosophy, or physical science, in schools which offer them training most broadly and most cheaply. And for you and me the lesson, not of such easy satire only, but of every living word of a loving God, is that what we read or study is to be that which sooner or

later will make us better soldiers in his service.
Wide is the sweep of that service, indeed. It
may be to stand faithful among the faithless,
as Abdiel. It may be to go to tell the message
of his love and wisdom to the ignorant, like
Gabriel. It may be to be a guardian of the
weak, like Raphael. It may be to stand
guard at the gate and keep away disease and
pestilence, hatred and malice, from those we
love, to detect falsehood by its own ugliness,
and to know truth of our own nature, like
Ithuriel. It may be to be "God's eyes, that
run through all the heavens, or down to the
earth bear his swift errands," as was the service
of Uriel. It may be to crush and destroy his
enemies, as was the work of Michael. Or it may
be that we are of that chorus and company of
all saints who also serve although they stand and
wait. Be it where he will, we are in his service.
Choose what line we will, we choose to build
up his kingdom. We are on the side of God,
and throw in our lot and our endeavor with the
progress and purity of his world. Do not let
any sceptic pull you down from that high ambi-

tion.  Do not let any sneer make you afraid to assert a claim so grand.  Your voice, your pen, your kindness, your patience, your sympathy, and your help, shall be more able and more — as you rightly use and train these talents which are his gift — to open blind eyes and deaf ears, to make homes happy, and to make deserts smile.  You live for him and to his glory.

## IX.

## THE TRAINING OF MEN.

WHEN I was little more than a boy, I was presented to Mr. John Tyler, then President of the United States, and had the advantage of a few minutes' conversation with him. He advised me as to my route in a journey I proposed into Virginia. He said I should not find the aspect of a large population, to which I was used in Massachusetts, — that their peculiar institutions withdrew the laboring people and their homes to a distance from the highways. " Indeed," said he, " you will not see so much of the evidences of material wealth in any part of Virginia. But, if you will go into the valley of the James[1] River, you will see the great turning-places of our history. You will see Jamestown, where American history began ; you will see Yorktown, where colonial history ended ; you will see the birth-place or the resi-

---

[1] Pronounced " Jeems," by Old Virginia.

dence of Patrick Henry, of Washington, of Jefferson, and of Madison. In such associations as these, you will be less curious about traces of physical prosperity."

I then learned, boy as I was, a lesson which I have never forgotten. For President Tyler was supposed to be susceptible to compliment, and I was young enough to be in the mood to humor him. I bent forward to quote the beautiful lines by which Mrs. Barbauld truly describes the greatness of England.

I was on the point of saying,—

"Man is the nobler growth your realms supply,"

when it occurred to me, just in time, that at that moment the principal trade of Virginia was the exportation of men to the Louisiana sugar plantations. She did not really care quite so much, just then, for Washington or for Jefferson, as for the growth of men for other purposes. The men who were brought up on her corn were sold as soon as they were men for the labor of Louisiana. The quotation, therefore,—

"Man is the nobler growth your realms supply,"

was fatally and sadly true, in a sense other than
Mrs. Barbauld's; and, at the same moment, it
was a fatal exposition of the cause of that poverty in resources which the President was ac-
knowledging.  I bit my lip, said nothing, which
is always wise, and the President passed on to
some other views of Virginian greatness.  I
meanwhile had learned, so that I have remembered it since, the lesson of the folly and vanity
of compliment.

That was thirty-three years ago, — a third of
a century ago.  In that time, I have travelled
often in Virginia, and every time when I have
gone there, I have come home haunted with the
remembrance of this first conversation I ever had
with a President of the United States; and with
the lesson of the value of men in the world,
which, though neither of us meant it, was con-
veyed in it.  I have now come home from
Louisiana and Texas, from the deserts of the
Indian Territory and Kansas, saying just the
same thing, —

"Man is the nobler growth our realms supply;"

and convinced again, and more convinced than

ever, that all schemes of reconstruction are·hope-
less, all victories of armies idle, all natural lu*-
ury of climate a snare, and all mineral wealth
a delusion, unless you have men to use the victories, men to enforce the laws, men to enjoy the
climate, men to subdue the earth. Again I
learn the eternal lesson of the vanity of things,
where there is no master spirit to control things.
It is the lesson of the nothingness of Nature,
unless the child of God — unless man — takes
Nature in hand to tame her.

One sits at home in our dismal climate, one
sees the hand-to-mouth work of our farming, —
crops of granite and of ice for its only exports,
— and one sighs for·richer fields and warmer
skies. Then one travels to see those fields and
to enjoy those skies; and one hears the word
that God said to Adam in the beginning, that
he bade him subdue the earth. One learns that
the earth is nothing unless you have the men;
and one asks how and when and where the
noblest man — the child of God most godly — is
to be found and is to be trained.

When one finds that, he finds how the wilder-

ness is to be vanquished and the desert blossom
with the rose. He sees, in fact, what Isaiah
saw in prophetic rapture, that the desert re-
joices and the wilderness is glad, only when
they see the coming of the true Son of Man.

I. This is, of course, true, though you speak
of dollars and cents, of mere material wealth.
I need not show that land alone is not worth a
penny,—not though it were underlaid with gold,
not though it bore corn and olive and vine,—
until you can put men upon it to take its treasure in hand. True, the Old World people, when
they come over here, forget this, land at home
seems so precious. They wonder how we can
afford to give away homesteads to settlers, if
they will only please to take them. The lesson
has been a lesson which our Southern friends
have found it hard to learn,— that the poorest
land, if it had a thousand people to the square
mile, was worth a thousand times as much as
one of their plantation baronies without inhabi-
tants. It is rather a curious feature of the early
colonization of all our States, that the unwel-

come lesson had to be taught to all capitalists that land alone is as valueless as water alone, — an acre of desert land as an acre of desert water. It took long to persuade an earl or a duke, to whom an English king had given a principality as large on the map as England, that really his master had given him nothing. It took long to persuade the Virginia Company, to whom King James gave half a continent, and the Plymouth Company, to whom he gave the other half, that in truth he had given them nothing. A generation, more or less, taught them, as the same length of time taught the barons and the dukes, generally at some cost, that they would be wise to part, when they could, from the royal gift, and bestow it on any one who would take it. Crozat and Law learned the same lesson in Louisiana. With such experience, whoever looks an instant at the causes of wealth sees why this is so. Robinson Crusoe's lump of gold had no value, because on his island there were no men who had need of gold. And so the worth of any spot on the world's surface in the market depends on its ease of access, — on the use, that is, which can be made of it in the enterprises of men.

II. That is mere matter of the exchange. What interests us in our purposes is the quality of the men who hold any territory. How much of manliness is there in them? Or, speaking more simply, how godly are these men? How much is there in them of the spirit of the creating God? Tossed on different surges of the same ocean, at the same moment of the year 1620, were two ships working westward, — one to Virginia and one to New England. They met the same gales; they rejoiced in the same east winds; they reached their harbors nearly at the same time; a hundred people in each perhaps. Yes, but what is the quality of these men? How much muscle? how much brain? how much soul? To ask the last question is to ask, How much of God is there? how near to God are they? how high in the grade of men?

The vessel on the Southern voyage has a hundred negroes from the Guinea coast. They have been stolen by Dutch adventurers. They

are brought to do field-labor beneath the lash on
this James River. They have learned nothing;
they know nothing. As far as you can ever say
it of men, they believe nothing, remember nothing, and hope for nothing. They hardly know
there was a past. They hardly look forward to
a future. The other vessel, the "Mayflower,"
has a hundred English Independents, culled
from the best wheat of England, and trained
for twelve years in the midst of the best wisdom
of Holland. They are men who for an idea
have left home. For right and for God they
have come into the wilderness. They are men
who live for faith, for hope, and for love. I
need not make any calculation of the worth of
these two cargoes. I would leave it to any man
who is used to the work of colonization. I will
take the most cold-blooded estimate of any bro-
ker of land. Which will be worth the most in
the market, when ten years have gone by, — the
sands of Plymouth, with what are left of the hundred God-fearing men and women, or the rich
bottom-land of Virginia, beneath the compelled
labor of what are left of the hundred faithless
slaves?

There is a distinction, as we see at the very outset, in the quality of men.

III. So we come back to our real question, How are such godly men to be found and trained, — how, when, and where? I have less and less faith in that convenient modern theory which makes out the great gifts of godliness and manliness to be the native fruits of certain climates, or of particular physical geography. I do not see that the facts sustain the theory. For, in truth, very diverse facts are called upon, as the theory happens to require. If the inquiry is about Peter the Great, who raised a barbarous State to be a first-rate power, you are told that northern climates develop strong characters, and make royal men. But if the royal man, who has made a small State into a great one, happens to be Solomon in Palestine or Pericles in Athens, you are told that the luxury of the climate of the Mediterranean gave fine chance for exquisite physical development, and for the mental and moral gifts which to physical development belong. We in New Eng-

land hear a good deal of the simple and pure
virtues of the Northern races, because we happen to belong to those races, and do not dislike
to paint our own pictures. Of course, our position saves us from many temptations; but what
is the worth of virtue which has never been
tempted? When I think of such men as Tous-
saint, born in San Domingo; as Napoleon, born
in Corsica; as Washington, born in Virginia; as
Dante, born in Florence; as Alfred, born in England; as Epictetus, born in Phrygia; as Socrates,
born in Athens; as David, born in Bethlehem,
—I see that moral goodness or mental greatness
belongs to no one climate or set of circumstances
more than another. And, if you speak of special gifts, no man who has seen Mr. Webster
tame an unwilling audience and carry it along
with him, and has read how Demosthenes did
the same thing with the mob of Athens, will
believe that the gift of eloquence is a special
gift, either of the mountains of New Hampshire
or of the ripples of the waves of the Ægean
shore.

How, when, and where, then, are we to find

the most manly men, which is to say, the most
godly? We must not look in a particular soil
for them, as if they were ground-nuts or turnips,
nor along a particular isothermal line, as if they
were palm-trees or pines. Jesus Christ struck
the key-note of the answer, when he reversed
all superficial speculations by saying, " The last
shall be first;" "He that is least among you
shall be greatest;" "He that humbleth himself
shall be exalted;" "He that is least in the kingdom of heaven shall be greater than the prophet
who has the most popular surrounding, or than
the ascetic whose fasting is most severe." In
all such announcements, sometimes abruptly
paradoxical in form, the central truth is proclaimed that manliness is a moral quality, — that
it belongs to spirit and the empire of spirit. It
is not a matter of mental fibre or physical fibre.
It is not to be contracted for, as you contract for
the staple of the wool of a sheep, for the flesh
on the thigh of an ox, for the speed or bottom
of a horse, when you go to the breeder of those
animals to tell him what you want, or when he
undertakes to supply you. " All these things

ye should have done, but not have left the others undone."

The physiological discoveries of recent times have done a good deal to help us in these questions. At the least, they have confirmed the best instructions of the prophets and other spiritual teachers, whose boldest statements are now confirmed even by the anatomists. I said this was not a matter of mental fibre or physical fibre. Now, it is not long since the impression was very widely diffused, that mental training had the most intimate relation with moral force. People really thought that you could argue or prove your way into heaven. Because we do not see the mind, people have been very fond of speaking as if mere mental processes, — such as memory, imagination, and reasoning, — were in themselves somehow elements of original power and sources of real life. People have talked as if Lord Byron or La Place or Goethe or Napoleon, because of their wonderful mental faculty, had any more original power, any more chance for moral insight and moral victory, any more sway of circumstance. No one would have said this of a giant, or a man of strong muscle, — of Milo of Crotona, or of some seven-foot Kentuckian. But men did say it of mental giants and persons of strong reasoning faculty. They spoke as if such brilliant mental marvels had a better chance of knowing God and doing his will than some stupid old black man, who could neither read nor write nor reckon. All this folly ought to be set aside by recent discoveries as to the nature of mere mental effort. For it proves now that an effort of memory or a train of argument takes up bodily fibre, tires out and wears down the body just as much as running a race does, or striking at a ball. It is made almost certain, from mere physical observations, that the merely intellectual efforts belong with feats of bodily strength. The mere mind and the mere body are to be ranked together.

All this observation makes simpler and more interesting all the set of studies, which show how the man himself, the living soul, is to control the mind and to control the body. The theory of the Dark Ages and of the Fathers of the Reformation is exploded, which taught that the man would gain vital power if he only understood about the Vicarious Atonement, or if he committed to memory a theory of the Fall of Man, or if he said that he believed one or another theory of the Trinity. The training of the mind and the training of the body must henceforth be regarded as on the same plane. And all men who believe there is a soul, especially all who believe that this soul survives the body, will see that the man gains in strength in proportion as the soul of man subdues body and mind together. And it is made certain, for such questions as we are trying to solve, that if we only have manhood enough in the men and womanhood enough in the women, they will control body and mind, whatever climate or soil, latitude or longitude. They will become monarchs even of the wilderness, and will compel it to blossom.

Force inheres in moral quality. Mind and body are its tools, and nothing more. Now, because moral quality, and the finest moral quality, may appear anywhere among the chil-

dren of God, — may appear in " Uncle Tom," in
his cabin ; in Jeanne of Orleans, in her peasant's
hut ; in Grace Darling, on the lonely storm-beat
shore, — you must arrange the steps of promotion for everybody, you must arrange your universal training for everybody, keep watch and
ward that every child of God may have a chance
as good as the best. When the lily of the field
germinates, there must be no heavy slate-stone
over its head to throw it back into darkness for
ever, while tares and whiteweed are flaunting
all around in sunlight and air, and scattering
their pestilent seeds for the destruction of future
harvests. This is the distinct and central rule
of Christian civilization. Give every child of
God the best that you can give in the way of
training; let him share equally with all the others. No matter if he come rushing in at the
eleventh hour. If he have neglected, or if others of his race have neglected, all the golden
opportunities of dawn or glorious noon, still, for
all that, do you, who are only stewards of God's
bounty, give him the same penny that you give
to those who have wrought with you all day.

For he is God's child as well as they, and so has the unstinted, untaxed, uncompared treasure of the very fulness of God's love. This is the meaning of that parable.

And in this fundamental axiom of the life of a republic, that it must keep open to the top every line of promotion, is that remark confuted which we sometimes hear in whispers, that popular education is to be limited to the elements of learning only. People say in whispers what they are not so apt to say when they are candidates, that the State should only pay for reading, writing, and arithmetic. It should not pay, they say, for Greek and Latin, for history, and a knowledge of fine art, because these are for the few who can pay for them, while the elements only are for all. This heresy starts on the mistake that it is for their own good only that the State trains them. In truth, the State trains them for her own good, first of all. Then the heresy supposes that the few who can pay for the higher training are the few who need it. But no man can tell where or in what class of society Jenny Lind is to be born, or Florence Nightingale, or Robert Fulton, or Abraham Lincoln; and we must not risk the loss of any one who would help the world by withholding at the right time the right culture. For the State's sake, we must offer it open-handed to them all.

But there need be no real danger from this heresy, nor from any of the short-sighted heresies of the old schools of politics, which were bred in castes or classes. If we can bear in mind always that the whole object of the State, — of constitutions of government, of systems of education, — is to make men and women who deserve those names, all our questions will be answered easily. All law, all policies, must be subordinated to this training of the citizen. All social order and all its machinery must serve the same great aim. For instance, fine art, the picture-gallery, the opera and the theatre, systems of trade, tariffs, and commercial regulations, school systems and college systems, — all these at bottom must be administered and must be planned so that you may gain the highest possible quality of manhood and of womanhood in all your citizens. I read every day discussions of free trade and tariffs which make me sick. People argue as if the great object of our race were to make iron cheaper, or cotton cloth, or kerseys. You would think Magna Charta and the Bill of Rights and the Declaration of Independence, the American Revolution and the Civil War, had all been ordered that the price of calicoes might be low in comparison with the price of gold. Now, in truth, these great eras of human society, these martyr struggles of brave men, have had objects and results worthy of martyrdom. The State exists, and its methods are improved, with the one design, which is God's own design, of making manly men and womanly women. A true State adopts that system of revenue and protection which best develops and best educates every man, woman, and child born within her border.

So I hear the new Art Education of England praised, which gives to every boy who will opportunity to use rule, crayon, pencil, brush, and graver. I praise it. I hope we may see it here. But it is not because I care so much for the patterns of our calicoes or our paper-hangings. It is because, for the child of God born yesterday in a hovel, I would have ready the best possible training for his best development; that his soul and heart, his conscience and affections, the part of him which is infinite and immortal, may use the best tools child of God can use, and win the highest victory child of God can win: for this the State lays her designs.

Your whole political or social problem of reconstruction becomes thus a problem of moral education. That the land just now redeemed —a land which, though redeemed, is still a wilderness—may blossom with the rose. How shall that be? Never, but around the homes of womanly women; never, but beneath the spade-blows of manly men.

In the Old World, the Church timidly obeys the direction of the State in such affairs. It educates only a few choir-boys in Rome, because the Church needs no wider education. In other countries it goes further, as the temporal ruler may permit. But everywhere, outside of Switzerland, the reign of classes must be maintained and taught, as the English Prayer-book says,

"To do my duty in that state of life unto which it shall please God to call me." It is our higher blessing that with us the Church owns no earthly master. In the great work of bringing all to the stature of a perfect man, we know no let or hindrance. In that great work, where Christ leads the way, of making men and women to be more like God, we may follow freely. We call the halt, the blind, the deaf, and the dumb. We will teach them all, encourage them all, uplift them all. We will inspire them all, so that no man shall be content with the state of·life he is in to-day, but each man shall pray and strive to find himself nearer God to-morrow. We must consecrate them all, that no man shall say that any thing he has is his own, but rather that each man shall hold as a trustee for the highest good of all. The State will never be satisfied with any thing she has attained. She will always forget the thing that is behind; and, always looking forward for worship more free, for communion more intimate, and for faith more firm, she will lift men to higher duty and success more abundant. Such men are each worth a thousand Persian legionaries, worth a thousand frightened slaves. Those men live in the life of God. They breathe the spirit of God. They work with the help of God, beneath God's own direction. It is in answer to the prayers of women thus trained, and to the work of men thus inspired, that deserts, but just now discovered, become prosperous commonwealths, — that the prairie of yesterday is the harvest-field of to-day. Ah ! more than this : it will be when such men and such women control it, that the land just-now wasted by slavery, and trodden down, fulfils the promises which God Almighty seemed to write on it in its soil and climate in the very beginning.

And not till then !

It is rather more than half a century since this country, without knowing it, drifted into the great experiment of universal suffrage. The men of the American Revolution hardly dreamed of so bold a theory. They gave the suffrage only to those who had some permanent interest in the land. It was afterwards, by steps but little thought of, that the supreme power was

11

given in equal shares to each man who lived under our sky. So soon as the country knew what it had done, the shrewd good sense of the country compelled the better school-education of the people, — of all the people. On that wave we have been swimming for fifty years. I do not say nor think that we have yet done the best we shall do in the line of mental education. But I hope we are learning a better lesson yet. I hope we are learning that what the people must have, if the land is to live, is moral education as the basis and ruling power of the whole. We must resolve on manhood and on womanhood fit to use these athletic bodies and to direct these cultivated minds. The country must learn that this great word, "Education," means a great deal more than the training of men's wits. It means a great deal more than the training of their muscles. It means the training of the soul of man. Unless he is more than an athlete, unless he is more than a reader, writer, or reckoner, he is not fit to be trusted with the use of such instruments as body or mind. And the State will perish if it rely on his suffrage, or that of men like him.

For this moral training the Church, in its thousand organizations, is of course responsible. Yet the cool good sense of the people has been right in its demand that the ordained officers of the Church — meaning its formal functionaries — shall not interfere in the day-schools, lest they carry there their professional jealousies and bigotries: so much more religious, at the bottom, is the whole people, than any one clan or section is apt to be. This exclusion, however, does not mean that the work of a common school, though it were a school for reading, writing, and arithmetic, shall not, first, last, and always — top, bottom, and middle — be devoted to making the boys manly and the girls womanly, — devoted all through to their moral training. It is the wisdom from on high which the land is after, and must have, if it is to be a nation. This wisdom is first pure, then peaceable and gentle; it is full of mercy and good fruits; it is without partiality and without hypocrisy. No wisdom is good for any thing which does not include this wisdom. And the schools and colleges are not worth even what the men are paid who sweep their floors, if they do not inculcate this wisdom through and through. The old statement about Harvard College— if it be still true, as I hope it is, in the profoundest sense of the words — is founded on a complete appreciation of what a college is for. "It is not so much," men used to say half a century ago, "what things the college teaches, or what it does not teach. It is that it takes in every year fifty cubs, and sends out every year fifty gentlemen." If the gentleman be a gentleman according to St. James's standard, or St. Paul's, one could have no higher description of the work of a college.

But I should have very little hope for the real moral education of the land, if I supposed it must be left on the chances of the schools of the land. When, with their eyes open, our fathers took the government of America out of the hands of the House of Brunswick, and took it on themselves, they really pledged themselves to God Almighty that the people of this land should, in every public ordinance and organization, be trained in their eternal life, — trained to be kings and priests, as the Bible squarely puts it. In point of fact, a high-toned town meeting or ward meeting, under the true government of a republic, is a school for the higher life, in which every day-laborer, sweating from the forge or dirty from the spade, may be lifted to higher life and conscientious duty. The theatre, when you can have stockholders or other owners who had rather die than that the State should suffer harm, may be made, often is made, a nurse for morals and the eternal life, whose successes any single church may envy. A high-toned journal, which would rather sink with its colors flying than wound a boy's purity, or puzzle an innocent girl by a coarse word, is one of the voices which, if only by its steady iteration, finds a way which no oracle could command. Then there are such lessons as those of Starr King, Orville Dewey, Wendell Phillips, and Waldo Emerson, in the lecture-room. A thousand people do not go to their homes after they have been hushed and entranced for an hour under the spell of one of these magicians, without seeing something of

the higher life; yes, and entering where these
men point the way. Such are some of the
methods of the moral training of this people
which their own good sense, working under the
inspiration of a present God, have appointed
and created. Thank God, then, the beginning
need not be made! But if this nation is to
endure, if this country is to be a country worth
living for and worth dying for, it needs vastly
more than a beginning. This country needs to
learn through and through, — from the President and Governor at one end, round to the
meanest pauper, whose taxes are paid for him by
a liquor dealer, at the other end, — that behind
and beneath its education in fine art, music, or
drawing, geography, geology, history, reading,
writing, and arithmetic, is its training in manhood and womanhood, its moral education. As
Mr. Speaker Long said so well the other day, a
prison must be a place where the man who stole
must be taught not to steal; the man who drank
must be taught not to drink. A Board of
Overseers of the Poor must be a board which
shall make unmanly men manly, and make

unwomanly women womanly.    Excises are to
be collected and tariffs levied on the principles
of social life which shall best train men and
women.    Amusements are to be licensed or repressed, liquor is to be bought and sold, public
lands are to be given away, emigration to be
encouraged or repressed, on systems which shall
make men and women purer and nobler.    Government is to learn that this is what government
in the end is for.    It is not to make people rich.
It is not to make them comfortable merely.    It
is to make men who are worthy of the name of
man, and women who are worthy of the name
of woman.

And we have all seen small communities,
where we were close enough to the work of
training to know that this was done, and to
know how it was done.    It has been well said
of our small country towns, that they train the
men and the women who are to lead the Bostons
and the Chicagos.    Where a whole community,
led by its best members, rises in protest against
every nuisance or cause of injury; where every
widow and orphan become the wards, so to

speak, of the tenderness of the whole; where society, almost of necessity, envelops and involves poor and rich, high and low, in one small and simple coterie or organism, — then good has its own chance to overcome evil, and light its own chance to dispel darkness. What a well-led village does, really so simply, is model or suggestion for what a great city might try for, and what, with its thousand advantages, it might attain, in some points, better than the little village. It does not become us who live in cities to fall in with the old complaint that they are always dangers to the common weal. In the outset of modern history, cities were the birthplace of freedom.

We never come to any crisis in history — a war, a conflagration, or a great election — without wishing that we had done more in this work of training men; without grieving for the chances we have lost, and rejoicing for the chances we have used. I heard a wise man from the West say last week that the tie which held the West to the East when the war came was, first of all, the result of the care with which the East had built Western schools, churches, and colleges. I know that a year ago no man was sorry that he had helped honest men establish their homes in Florida. Your crises in Washington — of silver, of greenbacks, of electoral colleges, of reconstruction, or of secession. — all set you back to wishing, not that the nation were stronger in wealth, not that it were more highly educated in letters or in arts, but that it had more good men and women, that it had higher moral training.

And the promise of the Saviour to his own was simply that they should triumph, because, as he said, they rested on the rock. "Your Father shall give you the kingdom." You are not to fear unless you lack in moral force. For all things are added to the moral power which that little flock supplies. At what moment it allies itself to the arm of flesh, it fails; as in Italy the Church has failed because it chose to rule by soldiers and by statesmen. At what moment it allies itself to the arts of the intellect, it fails; as all Protestantism has always failed when it relied on its logical systems or its syllogisms. But where and when it relies on truth, justice, righteousness, love, — then and there it succeeds. Other things round it crumble, burn to ashes, or blow away in dust; but the pure gold stands. The land which trains its people in such eternal life endures. It is to such a land that God gives the kingdom.

## · X.

## EXERCISE.

TWO friends are in a boat in the Mozambique Channel. A sudden flaw of wind upsets the boat. Before they can right her, she fills with water, and sinks ; and the two men are swimming for their lives. "Ah, well!" says one of them to the other, " it is a long pull to the shore ; but the water is warm, and we are strong. We will hold by each other, and all will go well." — " No," says his friend. " I have lost my breath already : each wave that strikes us knocks it from my body. If you reach the shore, — and God grant you may ! — tell my wife I remembered her as I died. Good-by! God bless you!" and he is gone. There is nothing his companion can do for him. For himself, all he can do is to swim, and then float, and rest himself, and breathe ; to swim again, and then float, and rest again, — hour after hour, to swim and float, swim and float, with that steady, calm determination that he will go home.; that no blinding spray shall stifle him, and no despair weaken him, — hour after hour, till at last the palm-trees show distinct upon the shore, and then the tall reeds, and then the figures of animals. Will one never feel bottom ? Yes, at last his foot touches the coral, and with that touch he is safe.

That story that man told me.

Now, what is the difference between those two men ? Why does one give up the contest at once, and resign himself to what people call his fate, while the other fights the circumstances for hours, and wins the battle ? On shipboard one was as strong as the other ; he was as brave ; he was as prudent as the other. " What if he were ? " you say. Strength and bravery and prudence were all needed in the crisis ; but something else was needed also. The man had never trained himself to swim. He knew how to swim, if knowing a method were of much use, where one has not trained himself to the habit. But that training he had never given.

Take that as a precise illustration, where no-body questions the answer, of the difference wrought in two men merely by exercise, or the steadiness of training. In matters like this, of pure bodily exercise, everybody sees and owns its work and its result.

We are beginning in our time to acknowledge the same work and the same results in other victories and in their companion failures. A country town sends two men to the legislature, — one because he understands all about the flowing of the meadows on their river, which is the great interest of that year; and another — well, because he has made a good speech at the town-meeting. But every one understands that the first is worth five times as much as the second, and that his opinion is of fivefold value. Yes, so it is, in a certain sense. But, when the great day comes, when that meadow business is to be explained to the House, our solid friend, laden with facts and figures, tries to explain it; and he begins at the wrong end. He takes for granted just what the House does not know, and he tells them just what they do know. He

empties the hall; and he sits down, with his
speech only half spoken, ready to weep for
mortification. It is then that his fresh, good-
natured, ready colleague whispers him out into
a committee-room, takes the manuscript of the
unspoken speech, and reads it; fixes in his mind
the four essential things, and makes sure that
he is not confused about them; goes back into
the House; waits till the right moment; and
then, just before the debate is closed, speaks for
ten minutes only. And then, all this which
was so dull becomes interesting to us all, and
that which was so obscure becomes perfectly
clear; and the whole business of the meadows
is set right for a century. What is the difference between those two men? You have to
confess there, that training, thorough exercise,
applies not only to swimming and fencing, and
playing the piano, and other matters of muscle
and nerve, — it applies also, it seems, to memory
and reasoning and imagination. It gives this
young fellow confidence and presence of mind
in face of an unfriendly audience, just as it
gave the other confidence and perseverance in

face of blinding spray. Whatever memory is, whether it be, as I suppose it is, simply a mechanical adjustment of fibres of the brain, or whether it be some inexplicable process of the spirit, — whatever the faculty of reasoning is, and whatever the faculty of the imagination is, — you find on any field-day, when the several recruits of God's army are reviewed, that those who have been exercised or drilled in the use of their faculties are, in that very training, the superiors of those who have let such drilling or exercise go by.   And so of other mental powers.

It is when we leave the domains of reasoning, of memory, or imagination, and come into lines of life even more difficult, if they be more familiar, that people begin to talk wildly, and fail to understand what one of the masters meant when he spoke of those " who have their faculties trained to the knowledge of good and evil."   Granted that swimming must be learned ; granted that the arts of the orator must be learned.   Yes ; but people say, carelessly, that every man knows the difference between right and wrong; and therefore it is said

there is no need of training there. "We are
outside the domain of the body," it is said.
"We are in the impalpable and viewless domain
of the spirit." Impalpable and viewless, —
granted; but not without law because viewless
and impalpable. The great law of life comes
in there as everywhere, that "practice makes
perfect," and that nothing else makes perfect.
It is not enough to know the right. That poor
fellow who sank in the Mozambique Channel
knew how to swim; but he had not that steady
familiarity with the water, and that godlike
confidence in his own power, which comes from
practice in swimming, and from that alone.
That worthy man who broke down before his
audience knew what he wanted to say; nay, it
was all written on the paper in his hand; nay,
between his tears of mortification, he could tell
it all to the other when they retired. What he
wanted was not the knowledge of the thing, but
practice, habit, and experience in saying it.
And these simple illustrations are enough to
show how fatuous and short-sighted is the cool,
off-hand statement which says, that, because we

all know the right, we shall, of course, equal each other in our capacity for doing it in an emergency.

Dr. Watts struck on the true statement when he described those

> " Who know what's right; not only so,
> But also *prac*-TISE what they know."

One of our most distinguished teachers, the late Francis Gardner, said, that in the case of two thousand or more boys who had passed under his care, no parent forgave him if he said, " Your boy is not quick or bright; but he is thoroughly pure and true and good." They did not forgive him for saying so, because they took it for granted that the goodness could be attained in any odd hour or so ; but the brightness or quickness seemed of much larger importance. On the other hand, if the teacher said, " Your boy learns every lesson, and recites it well; he is at the head of his class, and will take any place he chooses in any school," nine parents, he said, out of ten, were satisfied, though he should have to add, " I wish I were as sure that he were honest, pure, and unselfish. But in

the truth the other boys do not like him; and I
am afraid there is something wrong." To that
warning, he said, people reply, " Ah, well, I was
a little wild myself when I was a boy. That
will all come right in time." " Will come
right," as if that were the one line of life which
took care of itself, which needed no training ;
the truth being, that this is the only thing which
does *not* come right in time. It is the one thing
which requires eternity for its correction, if the
work of time have not been eagerly and carefully, and with prayer, wrought through.

When, then, we say, as we have to say so
often, that one of two men has been taken for a
higher preferment, has been promoted to a nobler career, and that the other has been left, or,
so to speak, set aside, we are sure to find, if we
can only reach a high enough point of view to
look down on the map or ground-plan of the two
lives, that there has been a very sufficient " law
of selection," which has governed the taking or
the rejection. The man who learned to swim
has swum. The man who learned to speak has
spoken. And it is as true that the man who

has trained his conscience assiduously and loyally, as a man of honor does, is not tempted, no, not a hair's breadth, by any thing which untrained men call temptation. This is simply as a truly trained gentleman does not so much as think of the possibility of saying what is not true.

The truth is that exercise is just as essential in the creation of character or its preservation as it is in accomplishments, whether of mind or of body. In simpler times, this was owned in the forms of familiar language; and in such times daily " exercise " was the chief business of the man. King Richard, Cœur de Lion, did not expect to maintain his prowess without steady exercise in the arts which went to it. Because he rode well when he was a squire, he did not give up his daily exercise in riding when he was knight or when he was king. Because, the day he was knighted, he could strike his adversary's helmet in tilting, he did not suppose he could keep his hand in practice unless the steady exercise of the tilting-yard, regularly and of system, added to the education of his boyhood. What was at first a difficult accomplishment became thus an easy feat, then a matter of course, and, last, an unconscious habit or knack of hand, arm, foot, and eye. But he would have lost the habit had he lost the daily exercise.

This is just what they meant, therefore, in such simpler times, when they say that a man was a proficient in all manly exercise, or that he kept up his daily exercises of piety and prayer, or that he exercised himself in conversation, in argument, in poetry, or in oratory.

In our time, for better, for worse, we have undertaken to transfer the business of education from youthful and mature life, and throw it all upon children. A girl of seventeen tells you that she has "finished her education;" and a boy of fourteen tells you that he hopes to finish his next week, so that he may "go into a store."

If it be understood on all hands that this change is only a change in the use of that word "education," why, there is no reason to complain. In Milton's time, in Raleigh's time, education meant the steady unfolding of all that

there is manly in man and womanly in woman.
It was, therefore, steady advance from knowledge to higher knowledge, from capacity to
higher capacity, from life to higher life. It
meant the leading along the baby till he became
the quick, honest, and fearless boy; the leading
along the boy till he became the true, simple,
and modest youth ; the leading along the youth
till he became the hardy, brave, and unselfish
man ; the leading along the man till he could
put the stamp of age on what manhood had
mined ; and then it meant the leading along of
this ripened man from this life to another life
which is higher. That was what the word " education " used to mean. No harm, if we choose
now to apply it only to certain exercises of
childhood, of text-book, and of school-room, if
we are well aware that we have shifted its old
sense. Then we shall provide some other word
for a great necessity. The necessity is for boy,
girl, man, or woman to keep all of good that
they have gained, and to gain more. This necessity compels their daily exercise.

One would be glad to illustrate this in the

discussion of details, which would require more space than can be here given to them. This must be said, on the central principle involved, — we are all, in a large degree, slaves to what is called the "division of labor." The shoemaker, it is said, therefore, need know nothing of farming, nor the farmer of the making of shoes. To this division nobody will object, so long as it is held within its legitimate limits. But it certainly passes those limits, if it prevent any man daily from getting fair exercise in each of the three great subdivisions of human life. Each man must have, every day, exercise in bodily strength, in intellectual accomplishments, and in moral and spiritual life. He has no right to commit suicide of one set of faculties more than another. He has no more right so to live that his intellectual faculties shall die out of him, or his spiritual faculties shall die out of him, than he has to take the slow poison, or to strike the coward blow by which his bodily faculties shall die.

The life of each man must have, every day, its fair share of physical, of mental, and of moral exercise.  Retaining these great classes, you may subdivide them as you please.  You may take for your bodily culture your exercise in your garden and orchard, and in travelling to and fro, and leave to other men the building of your house and barns, and the cultivation of your food ; but full bodily exercise you must have.  Or I may take such branch of mental culture as l please, and leave to other men the rest.  They may study the stars, may discuss politics, may pore over past history, while I content myself with some simpler walk ; but *some* walk or other of mental culture I must have. So I may leave to other men their peculiar preferences in spiritual life.  They may sit wrapt in meditation on the unseen glories of an unseen God, while I am playing jack-straws on the floor with my children ; but some spiritual exercise, exercise of the affections, I must have.  There is no division of labor which will enable me to save my soul by proxy.

The definition of exercise, then, is a threefold matter ; and we are not to consider the subject as if it related simply to the gymnasium, or the training of the body.

I can only attempt this general classification, simply calling attention once more to the closeness of the relations which bodily exercise, mental exercise, and the exercise of the affections bear to each other. It is, of course, impossible to lay down rules for all readers.

The man whose daily vocation is active employment in the open air has his bodily exercise largely provided for. He needs to consider and plan rather for his exercises of mind and soul.

On the other hand, the man or woman whose constant duty is intellectual, who is engaged on books or figures, needs to plan out physical exercise with special effort ; and also must see all the time that, in the daily duty, there is room and chance for the exercises of faith, of hope, and of love.

" We do not pay much attention to arithmetic in our schools," said some Japanese gentlemen, not long ago. " We think arithmetic makes men sordid." Perhaps it does ; perhaps it does not. Whether it does or does not depends on the amount of "exercise" of the affections, which is mingled with the intellectual training.

Of the physical exercises, it is more pleasant to speak than it was twenty years ago. The war has called attention to the scandalous neglect of them which was prevalent before. This nation called together a chosen army of seventy-five thousand men when the war began. The advance on Bull Run proved that those picked men could only move six miles a day in their first advance upon their enemy; this after near three months of discipline in camp. Compare that against a well-authenticated story of the movement of one of Wellington's divisions, which, in twenty-four hours, marched sixty miles in Spain; or compare it with Gen. Ord's advance in the last week of the war, when Sheridan telegraphed that, if things were pushed, the end had come. Grant replied, "Push things;" and then he pushed them.

Physical exercise is beginning to be expected of young men and young women. The time may come when it shall be respectable for men and women past thirty.

12

For persons whose daily business is sedentary, exercise of the body seems to come in more easily in the line of their amusements. Spirited games, in simple times and simple nations, filled out a great necessity. The illustration of the game of croquet, which keeps people in the open air, shows what such amusements can do. An Englishman's shooting and riding after the hounds have had a great deal to do with the fine physical health of the upper classes among the English. The constitution is inherited even by girls born from such fathers; and the taste for open-air exercise continues in the next generation, even with women who would consider it unwomanly to shoot, or, perhaps, to ride after the hounds. Cricket, as it is played by the cricket-clubs, is reduced to too solemn a game to be of much use as amusement or as exercise. But the cricket of a village-green, where there is not much science, and where there is a great deal of fun, answers a much better purpose. Base-ball has much more amiable qualities. With us, it is just now being ruined by the American extravagances, which make it what people call a "sporting game," a game of "professionals," as the popular slang calls them. Still, we ought not to permit the gamblers to drive us from an amusement which is our right. The fair development of this game is doing a good deal to rescue open-air amusements from their degradation.

Women have not paid as much attention to base-ball as perhaps they will. A great master in open-air games tells me that our women do not know the resource and amusement, for country or for indoor life, of battle-door and shuttle-cock. He tells me that there are, at least, eight varieties of this game, some of them highly complicated, which may be played by a party of thirty people together. It has, of course, the great advantage of giving thorough exercise to chest, neck, and arms.

The same advantage is to be found in sweeping: if the windows of the room be open, the exercise of sweeping can hardly be rivalled. I am not sure whether I am to speak of it as amusement. It is certainly recreation.

Mr. Nathaniel Parker Willis, who, with a very delicate constitution, led a literary life, and maintained himself in active pursuits, gave his verdict for horseback riding as the physical exercise most profitable for literary men. It gives air, chance for command, and exercise for lungs and arms. No one who thoroughly enjoys riding will dissent from him; but there are those who do not enjoy it. There is also one serious drawback on it which affects many of us, namely, that it always requires the existence and presence of a horse. Granting the horse, the horseman or horsewoman needs also a companion; for there is danger that the solitary horseman will carry his ledger with him in the front of his head and repeat his calculations as he rides, or turn over again that ugly letter which he received from a disappointed correspondent, or plan out for the tenth time the closing argument by which he is to reply to the defendant's counsel after they have closed. Granting the horse, granting good companionship, granting a good seat, and a pleasant day, a horseback ride certainly does unite all the requisites for healthful exercise.

Military drill stands very high among the various manly exercises. If the women secure the ballot, of course it will rank among womanly exercises; for it is very clear that no one should give a vote which, when the time comes, she is not prepared to defend. The special advantage is that the tired brain rests almost wholly, while the manual of arms, or the marching under orders, goes on. The recruit is wholly free from responsibility. I recollect the short periods of my own military service as periods of almost complete rest, though I was in high bodily activity. Such a comfort for an hour, or indeed for a series of hours, to have another man take the weight of direction! In the ancient systems of Greece and Rome, as in the training of Richard and of Raleigh, these exercises found important place.

The various schools of gymnastic exercises may safely be left to explain their own processes, — the heavy weights, the light weights, and the German gymnasia. This is certain, that all arrangements should be as social as possible; and that the arrangements which most resemble those of a family, bringing together all ages and both sexes, are, so far, the best of all. And let

us avoid the exaggerations which the teachers
fall into.  What we want is rightly to divide
effort, that spirit, soul, and body may be trained.
In the lives of most of us, great promptness and
celerity are the qualities most desirable.  As I
once heard Mr. Starr King say: " I do not want
to lift eight hundred pounds ; I never did want
to.  I do not want to be trained to draw three
tons on the high road.  What I want is to be
able to go at 2.40."

Mr. Webster, who was a great worker, used
to say that he could do more in six hours than
he could in eight.  He meant that, by rightly
throwing in two hours of exercise in the open
air, — fishing in the bay at Marshfield, or following a trout-brook at Boscawen, — he could
make the remaining six hours of more use than
all the eight together.  That system was the
secret of the Greek and Roman physical training.  Physical training was not a thing for boys
alone, but for men, and, in Sparta, for women
also.

In our climate, and in all climates milder than
ours, swimming, for the season when it is prac-

ticable, seems the exercise most efficient for men and for women. I believe it is still against the law for any person to go into the waters which wash the city of Boston. But as the city has provided bathing-places in which a hundred thousand people freely bathed last year, I suppose we may consider that ordinance virtually repealed. And we who live in Boston must look on the arrangement most gratefully, as the beginning of a system for hearty and sensible physical exercise of the people.

To speak of mental exercises in detail is to go over the whole compass of study involved in liberal culture. To discuss such "exercises," retaining the use of the word as it would have been familiar to Raleigh or to Milton, is the work not of the end of an essay, but of a volume.

Such a discussion I hope to enter upon — although only in an elementary way — in the next volume of this little series.

THE END.

# IN HIS NAME.

## A Story of the Waldenses, Seven Hundred Years Ago.

### By E. E. HALE.

### Square 18mo.   Price $1.00.

## A NILE JOURNAL. By Thomas G. Appleton. Square 12mo. Cloth. Price $2.25.

" The account furnished by Mr. Appleton of his winter on the Nile will probably be pleasant reading to those who have already passed through the same scenes. It gives a vivid photograph of that wonderful East, for whose shores we all have a reverent longing. The journal, kept by a man of varied experiences, and large and many-sided intelligence and knowledge, cultivated by travel and study, is a far better way of conveying even to the casual reader a real picture of what is most striking and characteristic than a mere dry recital of facts and figures, such as can be pieced out of guide-book and professed histories. It is by his skill in selection that Mr. Appleton has made a book that is especially rich in local color. Instead of giving a learned catalogue of the most striking remains, he furnishes a well-digested reference table of the books best worth reading. There is little of statistics, less of the frequent discussion of the questions of Eastern politics, nothing at all of Egyptian industry, but there is a glowing word painting of the scenes daily opened to a watchful traveller ; and, when prose fails, poetry serves to fill in the needful touches that make the picture perfect." — *Philadelphia Ledger.*

" We cannot follow this genial author any further. While we don't find any thing very heroic or daring in going down a well-known river in a canoe, we find a great deal that is of surpassing interest. He sees with the eye of an artist, and therefore always seizes upon the most salient points. He never tires us; and, when we have read on to the end of his book, we wish there were more, or that another book in the same vein would soon make its appearance." — *San Francisco Evening Bulletin.*

## A SHEAF OF PAPERS. By T. G. A. Square 12mo. Cloth. Gilt top. Price $1.50.

" These initials will be readily recognized as those of one of our best-known Boston wits, many of whose quaint sayings have already become proverbial. . . . In them [the papers], every reader will recognize a strong basis of common sense, a lively fancy, and a keen wit. The book is one to take up in any idle hour, and to put in one's pocket for a travelling companion ; and one cannot help wishing that the writer had also included in it some of the poems which were privately printed several months ago." — *Boston Transcript.*

" A very pleasant and thoughtful book, which we who are not of Boston do not like any less, but rather more, because it has an eminently Bostonish flavor ; and it affects us somewhat as 'a fine last century face.' These papers could not have been written from any other motive than the joy of writing them. They have an air of quiet about them that is wonderfully refreshing. Their talk of 'Art and Artists' is particularly pleasant." — *Christian Register.*

" He is one of the few Americans who have written too little, Mr. Emerson being the most conspicuous of that small band. A man of native wit, and now of world-wide experience, too little of which, perhaps, is practical, he cannot write otherwise than pleasantly, and often with a profound wisdom which takes on a superficial air only from the gayety of his style. He can write as lightly as a Frenchman, as seriously as a German, and yet with all his culture and his foreign anecdotes is simply an American, — even a Bostonian, — *malgré lui.*" — *Springfield Republican.*

*Sold by all booksellers. Mailed, postpaid, by the Publishers,*

## ROBERTS BROTHERS, Boston.

# REASON, FAITH, AND DUTY.

Sermons preached chiefly in the College Chapel.  By JAMES WALKER, D.D., LL.D., late President of Harvard College.  With a new likeness of Dr. Walker engraved expressly for this book.  Square 12mo.  Cloth.  Price $2.00.

---◆---

### *From the New York Tribune.*

The late President Walker is held in affectionate and reverent memory by a wide circle of pupils, and a numerous company of friends who were daily witnesses of the blended charm and energy of his character.  He was a man who made a deep impression on all with whom he came in contact.  The austerity of his intellect was combined with a gracious sweetness of demeanor rarely found together in the same person.  The leading feature of his nature was a sense of justice which in his mind was identical with a passion for truth.  This quality seasoned and animated the whole course of his life.

### *From the Unitarian Review.*

Dr. Walker was pre-eminently a preacher for preachers to study.  He was strong exactly where the usual pulpit style of address is weak ; and to this is to be ascribed the influence of his sermons over the very classes whom preaching finds most difficulty in affecting.  Young men full of impatience at the conventional, and quick to scorn shams and empty words, hung on his speech ; clear-headed and hard-headed business men recognized in him a master of the secrets of human nature ; souls of the most earnest piety found in his few simple words renewal and inspiration.

### *From the Boston Transcript.*

There can scarce be a religious person of any style or school, a philosopher even, or a moralist, or a simple lover of earnest, lucid, and vigorous intellectual power, given to didactic discoursing in preaching or in ethics, but will detect and own and feel the master's sway in this volume.

---◆---

*Sold by all booksellers.  Mailed, post-paid, by the Publishers,*

## ROBERTS BROTHERS, BOSTON.

.

# WAYS OF THE SPIRIT,

## *AND OTHER ESSAYS.*

BY

FREDERIC HENRY HEDGE, D.D., LL.D.

———◆●◆———

The Way of History; The Way of Religion; The Way of Historic Christianity; The Way of Historic Atonement; The Natural History of Theism; Critique of Proofs of the Being of God; On the Origin of Things; The God of Religion, or the Human God; Dualism and Optimism; Pantheism; The Two Religions; The Mythical Element in the New Testament; Incarnation and Transubstantiation; The Human Soul.

SQUARE 12MO.  CLOTH.  PRICE $2.00.

———◆———

*Sold by all booksellers. Mailed, postpaid, by the Publishers,*

ROBERTS BROTHERS, BOSTON.

# LAST SE.RIES

OF

# CHRISTIAN ASPECTS OF FAITH AND DUTY.

Discourses by JOHN JAMES TAYLER, Late Principal of Manchester New College, London. Square 12mo. Cloth. Price $2.00.

### From the Christian Register.

Twenty-six sermons, mostly preached within the last ten years of the author's life, are here selected and arranged by his daughter, who has been assisted by Rev. James Martineau. This is not a volume for sensation hunters, but for those who hunger and thirst after righteousness. The high and serious mind of John James Tayler could treat no pulpit theme except with reference to the deep and unutterable wants of the human soul. He welcomes "every new discovery of science, and every fresh result of scholarship, as phenomena which themselves become religious through the light cast on them by the soul." He thus puts all nature in harmony with "the spirit of Christ, whose image is ever before him as an embodiment of true religiousness." The volume fitly closes with a sermon on "The Immortal Future Mercifully Veiled to Us by God," — the last pulpit discourse of Mr. Tayler, who died in 1869, in his seventy-second year.

### From the Boston Globe.

Tender in their sympathy, gentle in their thoughtfulness, yet strong and brave in their assertion of the vital truths of religion and morality, these discourses are worthy of a place in the library of every Christian. Their breadth and liberality of tone show the high plane of endeavor which the author has sought and attained.

*Sold by all booksellers. Mailed, postpaid, by the Publishers,*

ROBERTS BROTHERS, BOSTON.

# QUIET HOURS.

## *A COLLECTION OF POEMS, MEDITATIVE AND RELIGIOUS.*

———◆———

"Under this modest title we have here about a hundred and fifty of the best short poems in the language. The compiler, whoever she is, has a rare taste, and also, what is equally valuable, good judgment. The poems are on all subjects. This dainty little volume is just the book for a Christmas or New Year's gift." — *Peterson's Magazine.*

"Such a book as this seems to us much better adapted than any formal book of devotion to beget a calm and prayerful spirit in the reader. It will no doubt become a dear companion to many earnestly religious people." — *Christian Register.*

"'Quiet Hours' is the appropriate title which some unnamed compiler has given to a collection of musings of many writers — a nosegay made up of some slighter, choicer, and more delicate flowers from the garden of the poets. Emerson, Chadwick, Higginson, Arnold, Whittier, and Clough, are represented, as well as Coleridge, Browning, Wordsworth, and Tennyson; and the selections widely vary in character, ranging from such as relate to the moods and aspects of nature, to voices of the soul when most deeply stirred." — *Congregationalist.*

———◆———

18mo, cloth, red edges. Price $1.00. Sold by all Booksellers. Mailed, postpaid, by the Publishers,

· ROBERTS BROTHERS,
*Boston.*

www.ingramcontent.com/pod-product-compliance
Lightning Source LLC
Chambersburg PA
CBHW030626030726
47497CB00006B/1654